FIVE
O'CLOCK
TALES

FIVE
O'CLOCK
TALES

Enid Blyton ™

EGMONT

EGMONT

We bring stories to life

First published in Great Britain 1941 by Methuen & Co Ltd
Dean edition first published 1991
Mammoth edition first published 1993
This edition published 2008
by Egmont UK Limited
239 Kensington High Street
London W8 6SA

ISBN 978 1 4052 3972 1

1 3 5 7 9 10 8 6 4 2

www.egmont.co.uk

A CIP catalogue record for this title is available from the British Library

Printed and bound in Great Britain by the CPI Group

CONTENTS

The Red and White Cow

Peter was most excited because his father and mother had moved into the country from the town. How different it was! There were green lanes instead of busy streets, big trees instead of tall chimneys, and *such* a lot of animals and birds to see.

'There are thirty-two sheep in the fields and six little lambs!' said Peter to his mother. 'And there are eleven horses at the farm, and I saw two goats this morning and about twelve ducks. I couldn't count them properly because they wouldn't stay still. The hens won't stay still either.'

'What about the cows?' said his mother. 'Have you counted those?'

'I don't like the cows,' said Peter. 'They have big horns and they roar at me.'

'Oh, no,' said his mother. '*Lions* roar. Cows only moo.'

'Well, it sounds just like roaring to me,' said Peter. 'I don't like the cows at all. They are my enemies.'

'They are very good friends!' said Mother. 'They send you a lot of presents.'

'*I've* never seen a present from a cow!' said Peter.

'Well, here is one,' said Mother, and she took down a jug of milk. She poured it out into a mug and gave it to Peter. He drank it.

'So that came from the cow, did it?' he said. 'Well, it was simply lovely!'

At dinner-time Mother put down a dish of stewed apples for Peter. He looked round for the custard that Mother usually made for him. There wasn't any.

'The cow has sent you this present instead!' said Mother – and she gave him a dear little jug full of thick cream. How delicious it was! Peter poured it all over his apples. They tasted much nicer than usual.

'So that came from the cow, too!' said the little boy. 'Well, it must be a very kind animal!'

At tea-time Mother put the loaf of bread on the table. Peter was surprised. Usually there were slices of bread and butter.

Mother put down a blue dish on which there were little rolls of new-made yellow butter.

'A present from the cow again!' she said, and laughed, 'You can spread your present yourself on slices of bread for a treat!'

'Goodness me!' said Peter. 'What a nice friendly creature the cow is! I won't hate it any more or be frightened of it.'

'I should think not!' said Mother. 'Look, Peter – the cow has sent *me* a present too!'

Mother lifted up the lid of the cheese-dish, and underneath Peter saw a big lump of orange-coloured cheese. Mother cut herself a piece, and said it was delicious.

'I shall go and stand on the gate that leads to the cow field and say thank you to the cows!' said Peter. 'I didn't know they were so kind!'

And now he isn't a bit afraid of them, and he likes them very much. He says they are his friends, not his enemies. What do *you* say?

The Clock in the Wood

Once upon a time three children went out to have a picnic. They were Bob, Mollie, and Eileen. They had a basket full of nice things to eat and a ball to play with. They waved goodbye to their mother and set off to Bluebell Wood.

'Please start back at five o'clock,' she called to them. 'Uncle Jim will be here then and he will want to see you.'

'Yes, Mother,' called back the children. 'We've got our watches!'

They soon came to Bluebell Wood. It was a lovely place. There were still some bluebells shining here and there like pools of blue water. The birds were singing in the trees, and the sunshine slanted through the green branches and made freckles of light on the grass below.

'Let's play hide-and-seek!' said Bob. 'We'll put the basket of tea things under this tree while we play. I'll hide my eyes first.'

When the others called 'Cuckoo', Bob ran to find them. He found Mollie – but as he ran after her he caught his foot in a tree-root and over he went! He didn't hurt himself, but, oh, dear, he broke the glass of his watch!

'Look!' he said. 'My watch is broken! Isn't it a pity! Is yours all right, Mollie? We must know the time to go home.'

'Yes, mine's all right,' said Mollie. 'Never mind, Bob – we'll soon get yours mended!'

'What's the time, Mollie?' asked Eileen. 'Is it time for tea yet?'

'It's four o'clock,' said Mollie. 'Yes – we'd better have tea.' So they fetched their basket and handed out the good things – tomato sandwiches, chocolate cake, and an apple each to eat. What a fine tea! There was nothing left at all except three paper bags and the milk bottle and cup when the children had finished!

'Let's have a game of catch now!' said Bob. So they began. It was great fun and they played for a long time. Then Bob wondered what the time was. He didn't want to miss seeing Uncle Jim! He looked at his watch. Oh, dear – it was broken! He had forgotten that. So he called to Mollie.

'Mollie, what's the time?' Mollie looked at her watch.

'Four o'clock!' she cried.

'But it can't be!' said Bob, surprised. 'You said it was four o'clock just before we had tea! Look again!'

Mollie looked – and then she held her watch up to her ear. 'Oh!' she cried in dismay. 'It's stopped. Now what shall we do? Eileen hasn't a watch! We can't tell the time!'

'I can!' said Eileen, suddenly. She ran to where a big dandelion plant grew and picked a big fluffy dandelion clock. She blew it hard. Puff! She blew again. Puff! Still there was some white fluff left. She blew again. Puff! That was 1 o'clock, 2 o'clock, 3 o'clock – puff, 4 o'clock, puff, 5 o'clock!

'It's five o'clockl!' cried Eileen. 'I've puffed all the fluff off. The dandelion clock says it's five o'clock – time to go home!'

'Come on then!' cried the others, and off they all went. Mother was so pleased to see them in such good time, for Uncle Jim had just come.

'It wasn't our watches that told us the right time!' said Eileen. 'It was the little clock in the wood, Uncle Jim!'

The Peppermint Rock

Mollie and John were very pleased because their Uncle Bob had given them a long stick of pink peppermint rock between them. He had been to the seaside for a day and had brought it back with him. It had 'Southsea' all through the middle of the rock in pink letters. Mollie did wonder how the name was put there.

'We'll break it in half,' she said to John. So she broke it – but one piece was bigger than the other.

'I want the big piece!' said John, and he snatched at it. But Mollie wouldn't let him have it. 'No,' she said, 'I'm the oldest of the family – *I* ought to have it.'

'Selfish thing!' said John and he smacked Mollie, which was stupid, because she at once smacked him back.

'Hello, hello, what's all this?' suddenly said a voice behind them. The two children turned and saw the butcher's boy. They did not like him very much, for he was rough and rude. But John told him what they were quarrelling about.

'It isn't fair, Harry,' he said. 'Look, Mollie has broken the rock into two – and she won't give me the bigger piece. Say *I* ought to have it!'

'I'll settle your quarrel for you,' said Harry. 'Give me the rock and let me measure the pieces.'

Mollie gave him the rock. The butcher boy measured them side by side, saw that one was a whole inch bigger than the other and bit off a large piece of the longer one! But he bit off too much, because when he measured the two pieces again, the piece he had bitten was now smaller than the other.

'Huh! I'll soon put *that* right!' said Harry, and he bit a large piece off the longer stick. Mollie and John stared in dismay.

'Don't do that,' begged Mollie. 'Give us the two pieces back. We won't quarrel any more.'

'Wait!' said Harry. 'I haven't got them right yet. One is still longer than the other. If I give you the pieces back like this you will squabble again! Another bite may set things right.'

He took another large bite, measured the

sticks, and, of course, found one still longer than the other. So he bit again, crunching with enjoyment. And now, alas! there were only two very small pieces of rock left, and the children were almost in tears.

'Give us those little bits,' said Mollie. 'You have no right to eat all our rock like that.'

'Oh, indeed!' said Harry. 'And what about my trouble in trying to settle your stupid quarrel for you? What reward do I get for that? Aren't you going to give me anything for trying to put things right?'

'We've nothing to give you,' said John.

'Well, if you think a big boy like me, who earns his own living, is going to settle your quarrels for nothing, you're mistaken!' said Harry. 'I'll take my own payment – the rest of this peppermint rock. Goodbye!'

And with that he crammed the rest of the rock into his mouth and went off grinning. The two children watched him go, with tears in their eyes.

'It's our own fault, John,' said Mollie. 'If one of us had been unselfish enough to take the smaller piece, we wouldn't have lost the lot!'

Brer Fox's Onions

It happened once that Brer Rabbit passed by an onion field and saw Brer Fox hard at work digging in it.

'Heyo, Brer Fox!' he called. 'Are those your onions?'

'They are,' said Brer Fox, 'but it's mighty hard work digging this hot day.'

'Well, I'll come and help you,' said Brer Rabbit, and he hopped into the field and began digging up the onions too. They were nice little round onions, and Brer Rabbit thought of them in hot soup. Ooh, delicious! He felt sure Brer Fox would give him a good handful for helping him – but no, when Brer Fox stopped, he didn't say a word about Brer Rabbit having any onions at all. He took up a small sack nearby and began to shovel the onions in.

'Aren't you going to give me a few?' said Brer Rabbit, in a rage.

'No, not one,' said Brer Fox, grinning. 'You've tricked me a good many times, Brer Rabbit, and I don't feel very kindly towards you. You don't even get the smallest onion!'

Brer Rabbit stood and watched Brer Fox for a minute. 'That sack's too small for all those onions,' he said. 'I'll lend you a bigger one. I don't bear *you* malice, Brer Fox. I do a kindness when I can.'

Brer Fox laughed loudly at that, but all the same he accepted Brer Rabbit's offer of a large sack. Brer Rabbit fetched it – but when he helped Brer Fox to hoist it, full of onions, on to his back, he took a knife and quickly cut a nice little round hole at the bottom of the sack! Then he grinned, said goodbye to Brer Fox and went off, lippitty-clippitty. But he didn't go far. No, he soon came back, picked up the small sack that hadn't been used, and set off down the road after Brer Fox, who by now had turned the corner. Brer Rabbit didn't need to ask the way he had gone, for there, all down the lane, was a string of little round onions that had dropped one by one from the hole in the sack!

How he grinned to himself! He picked them all up and put them into his sack. Then round the corner he went after Brer Fox and saw another line of onions. Into his sack they went too, and when it was full he turned and ran home to his wife. 'Make some onion soup!' he shouted, and flung down the sack.

And when Brer Fox reached home, and put down *his* sack, what a shock for him! Only a few onions were in the sack – all the rest had gone! He ran out and looked down the road! Not an onion was to be seen! He rushed to Brer Rabbit's house, which was fast bolted – but out of the window stole a most delicious smell of onion soup.

'Have some?' cried Brer Rabbit, leaning out of his window and waving a soup spoon at Brer Fox. But Brer Fox, he didn't answer a word!

There and Back Again!

Bob emptied the pennies out of his money-box, It was Mollie's birthday the next day, and he meant to buy her a book. He had two pounds altogether, so off he went to the bookshop. He saw there a book he wanted very badly himself – *Tales of Brer Rabbit* – and he felt sure Mollie would like it. So he bought it, and left the parcel at Mollie's house with a kind little letter.

Now, Mollie was a very naughty little girl. She was spoilt and disobedient, and on her very birthday morning she did three bad things. She poured all the milk from the milk jug into the teapot; she broke a vase of flowers; and, worse of all, she threw a stone at a cat and hurt its leg. So her mother said that, even though it was her birthday, Mollie must be punished. She took the *Tales of Brer Rabbit* away from the naughty little girl, and said she would give it away.

So the lovely book was given away to the

milkman's boy – but when he got home and looked at it he found that it was just the same book as he had already had for Christmas. He was disappointed – but never mind, he would give it to Alan, the little boy across the road, who had been ill.

So the milkman's boy wrapped up the book and left it at Alan's house with a message. His mother unwrapped the parcel – but when she saw it was a book she wouldn't give it to Alan. The doctor had said that her little son must *not* read at all, because his eyes were very bad – so his mother had carefully kept every book out of his bedroom. He was fond of reading, and she felt sure he would find the new book somehow if she kept it.

She wrapped it up again – and then she thought of Alice, the little girl who lived with her grandmother in the next street. Alice would like the book very much. She put on her hat and ran to the house. She left the book there and ran home again.

The grandmother was surprised when she opened the parcel and found the book – but dear me, Alice had gone far, far away! She had left on a steamer for Canada, where her father and mother were, and was not coming back till she was grown-up. The old grandmother wondered whom she could give the book to.

'There's that kind little chap, Bob,' she suddenly thought, 'When Alice was ill he came to see her every day. He always sent her a card for Christmas and often asked her to tea, because her mother and father were so far away. I'll send it to *him*!'

And *how* surprised Bob was when the book he had bought came back to him! He was *so* pleased – and I think he deserved it, don't you?

Snapdragon Snippets

The Snippet Pixies lived in the mushroom fields, where houses were cheap. As soon as a fine mushroom grew up the Snippets snipped out a door and a window, made a stairway inside the stalk and a room inside the mushroom top, and hey, presto! there was a house big enough for two Snippets at least!

But one day it happened that a boy came along who saw the mushrooms and picked them – and, dear me, what a surprise for him when he saw the doors and windows! The Snippets flew out at once and fled away from the field. The boy followed in glee. He thought they were butterflies or moths, and as he carried a net with him he meant to catch them.

The Snippets flew on and on, panting hard. They flew over a cornfield and the boy rushed after them. They flew down the lane, they flew

through a wood, and at last, quite tired out, they flew into a garden.

'We can't fly any further!' panted one little Snippet, sinking down to the ground like a tiny bubble. 'That boy will have to catch us!'

'What's the matter?' asked a bumble bee near-by.

The Snippets told him. 'There's the boy, look, coming in at the gate now!' they groaned. 'Whatever can we do? There doesn't seem any-where to hide, bumble bee.'

'Quick! I'll show you a place!' buzzed the velvety bee. 'Follow me!'

He flew to a red snapdragon. He alighted on the lower part and pressed it down so that the snapdragon opened its 'bunny-mouth'. In went the bee – and the mouth of the snapdragon closed behind him so that not even a leg could be seen! He pushed himself out backwards to the surprised Snippets.

'There you are! Get inside any of these snap-dragon flowers and you'll be well-hidden!'

The Snippets gave little high squeals of glee. Each one flew up to a red, pink, or yellow snapdragon, and pressed hard on the lower lip of the flower. The mouth opened – the Snippets slipped in – the mouth closed up! Not a wing was to be seen, not even a tiny bare foot!

The boy banged the garden gate and looked round. 'Where are those strange little butter-flies?' he said, holding his net ready to catch them. 'I know they flew into this garden, for I saw them. Where have they hidden them-selves?'

He went to the flower-bed. He set the flowers swinging to and fro, so that he might frighten any butterfly into the air. But the Snippets were safe, though their hiding-places swung about as the boy pushed them with his net. It was like being in a cosy hammock. The flowers smelt lovely, too – they made a wonderful hiding place!

The boy soon left the garden, and it was safe for the Snippets to come out. They peeped from their strange hiding place and nodded to one another. 'We can't go back to our mushroom houses now,' they cried. 'Shall we live here instead?'

Everybody thought it was a good idea. They went to buy soft yellow blankets for beds from the gnome under the hedge, and that was all they needed. Each night they crept into the bunny-mouths of the snapdragons and slept on their hammocks of yellow down, and they probably do still.

You won't find them there in the daytime, for then they are at work snipping up fallen flower petals to make frocks and coats – but you might press open a snapdragon gently and see if you can find the Snippets' downy yellow beds made ready for the night!

Oh, No, Brer Fox!

One day Brer Bear gave Brer Rabbit six fine pots of new honey, golden yellow and sweet. Brer Rabbit was very pleased. He put them in a basket and set off home. It was a hot day, and he sat down beneath a tree to have a rest. Soon his head nodded and he fell asleep.

It wasn't long before Brer Fox came padding by. He was just going to pounce on Brer Rabbit when he saw Brer Hare's ears sticking up behind a bush, watching him. So he thought he would take the honey instead. He picked up the basket and padded off with it, grinning away to himself.

Well, of course, Brer Hare told Brer Rabbit what had happened, and Brer Rabbit was as wild as could be! He sat and puzzled hard how to get back that honey. Then he slapped his knee and grinned.

Off he went, back to Brer Bear's again.

'That robber, Brer Fox, has stolen the honey you gave me, Brer Bear,' he said. 'But I'll get it back! Aha, I will! I've got my cousin, Brer Hare, coming in to talk to me tonight ● and we're going to plan how to get that honey back. Brer Hare's clever – and so am I – and between us we'll make a fine plan!'

Well, of course, when Brer Fox met Brer Bear that day, as Brer Rabbit had known he would, Brer Bear told Brer Fox what Brer Rabbit had said. Brer Fox rubbed his sharp nose and grinned, 'I'll be under Brer Rabbit's windowsill tonight listening to his plans!' he said.

Well, that night Brer Rabbit set his radio going, very low. There was a lot of talking on it. When he had set it just so, Brer Rabbit put on his cap and slipped outside under a bush. Presently along came Brer Fox, going as softly as a cat. Brer Fox sidled in at the gate and crept up to Brer Rabbit's windowsill. He crouched down there and listened hard.

'Brer Hare and Brer Rabbit are talking mighty quiet!' he said to himself. 'Maybe soon they'll talk up and I'll hear what they are planning.'

Brer Rabbit watched him and he grinned a

big grin all to himself. He went quietly out of the back gate and then set out for Brer Fox's house as fast as ever he could, lippitty-clippitty through the woods. When he got there he opened the door and went in. He looked round – and the first thing he saw on a shelf was his honey, neatly set out, six pots in a row. Brer Rabbit found his basket under the shelf, too, and he quickly popped all those pots into it.

He ran home – and he walked in at his gate as bold as brass, whistling loudly. Brer Fox heard him and stared in astonishment, for he had thought Brer Rabbit was indoors talking away to Brer Hare! Brer Rabbit switched on his torch and turned it on to Brer Fox under the windowsill.

'Heyo, Brer Fox!' he said. 'Still there! Well, well, well!'

'Where have you been?' asked Brer Fox, an awful thought coming into his mind.

'Been, Brer Fox? Oh, I've just been getting honey for my breakfast tomorrow!' said Brer Rabbit, skipping into his house before Brer Fox could catch him. He put his head out again and bawled, 'So glad you like my radio, Brer Fox! Come in some night and hear it again!'

The Top of the Wall

Old Man Greeneyes lived in a little cottage surrounded on all sides by a high red wall. He liked to be sheltered from the winds – and from prying eyes; for Old Man Greeneyes was half a wizard!

Next door to him lived Dame Fiddlesticks and her children. Dame Fiddlesticks was a most inquisitive person and loved to peep at her neighbours. If she went into her bedroom she could just see nicely over the wall into the old man's garden. That *did* annoy him! And then the children took to climbing on the top of the wall and calling to him. That annoyed him more than ever!

At last he decided that he must do something about it. If he had the wall made higher by a foot, and put some glass spikes on top, Dame Fiddlesticks couldn't see into his garden from her bedroom window and the children wouldn't be able to climb up and sit on top. So off he went to Mr Hod the builder.

'Yes,' said Mr Hod. 'It would be easy to do what you want – but you will offend Dame Fiddlesticks mightily. She might throw her rubbish over your wall in revenge, and her children would certainly call out after you when you go walking, for they are not very well-mannered. Take my advice and think of something else. It is usually just as possible to get your way in a kindly manner as in an ill-natured one.'

Old Man Greeneyes nodded his head and went to see his cousin, Mother Tiptap. She heard what he had to say and smiled. 'I've just the thing for you!' she said. 'See, here are some new seeds I have made. Plant them on the top of your wall and see what happens.'

'But no seeds will grow on a *wall*,' said Old Man Greeneyes. Still, he took them and planted them all along the top of his wall. Then he waited to see what would happen. The rain came. The sun shone. Those tiny seeds thrust out roots into the wall-crannies. They sent up small leaves. They grew and they grew.

And then one day in the springtime they

flowered into bright yellow and red – tall plants, over a foot high, with the most delicious scent in the world! Old Man Greeneyes smelt them from his kitchen window and was glad. Dame Fiddle-sticks feasted her eyes on them, for she loved flowers, and when she smelt their scent she was full of joy.

'Don't you dare to climb up on that wall any more!' she warned her children. 'I won't have those beautiful flowers spoilt that that kind old man has planted there. They've grown so high that I can't peep into his garden any more, but what does that matter? I'd rather see the flowers there!'

She was so delighted that she sent in a new cake she had baked to the old man. He went to thank her and asked what he could do in return for her kindness.

'Oh, if only you'd give me a few seeds of those lovely flowers of yours growing on the wall,' she said. 'What are they called?'

'They've no name at present,' said the old man, smiling. 'What shall we call them? Let's ask the children?'

The children knew what to call them, of course! Do *you* know the name?

A Busy Morning

There was once a little boy called William Robert, and his mother used to call him Billy-Bob for short. He was a useful boy, and did all sorts of things for his mother and father. He used to run errands every day, and he really had a very good memory indeed.

One day his mother said, 'Billy-Bob, please go to the grocer's and get me a packet of tea.'

'A packet of tea,' said Billy-Bob. 'Yes, Mother.'

As he went to the door his father said, 'Billy-Bob, please get me a box of nails.'

'A packet of tea, a box of nails,' said Billy-Bob. 'Yes, Daddy.'

As he went down the path, his aunt, who lived next door, called him. 'Billy-Bob, if you're going out, please get me a bag of buns for tea at our baker's.'

'A packet of tea, a box of nails, and a bag of

buns,' said Billy-Bob to himself. 'Yes, Auntie.'

He was just going out of the gate when his uncle came up on his way home. 'Hello, Billy-Bob,' he said. 'Are you off shopping? Here's fifty p. Buy me a paper, there's a good boy.'

'A packet of tea, a box of nails, a bag of buns, and a paper,' said Billy-Bob. 'Yes, Uncle.'

He went down the road. Old Mrs Brown knocked on the window when she saw him passing. 'Billy-Bob!' she called. 'Please get me a pot of cream and a quarter of peppermints, will you?'

'A packet of tea, a box of nails, a bag of buns, a paper, a pot of cream and a quarter of peppermints,' said Billy-Bob. 'Yes, Mrs Brown!'

On he went, and met Mr Jones. 'Hello, Billy-Bob!' said Mr Jones. 'Are you passing the fish shop? Please buy me a nice kipper, will you? Here's the money.'

'A packet of tea, a box of nails, a bag of buns, a paper, a pot of cream, a quarter of peppermints, and a nice kipper,' said Billy-Bob to himself. 'Yes, Mr Jones.'

He went on. Soon he met Jim and Peter, and they showed him their new marbles. Then he met Susan and she told him how she had fallen down, and showed him her bandaged knee. Then after that he met Tom, who gave him a sweet and told him that his mother had made some ginger buns for tea.

'I must hurry!' said Billy-Bob to himself. He went to the grocer's and bought – well what *did* he buy? He went to the ironmonger and bought – can you tell me? He went to the baker's, and what did he get there? He went to the dairy and came out with – what? He went to the sweet shop and put down the money for – can *you* remember? And last of all he went to the fish shop, and there he asked for a nice – do *you* know what it was?

What a lot of parcels he had! Off he went home, and on the way he repeated the list over to himself – and, dear me, Billy-Bob had forgotten something! Yes, he had! What could it be, oh, what could it be? Yes – you are right – he had forgotten his uncle's paper! He met a newsboy and bought one. Now Billy-Bob was happy. He ran off home, carrying seven things – and who can tell me what they were?

The Witch's Egg

Once upon a time Sneaky the elf peeped into Witch Upadee's kitchen and saw her working a spell. First she took a small chocolate Easter egg and put it on a plate. Sneaky knew the kind. You could buy them for twenty-five p each, and they were filled with sticky cream inside. He sat himself on the windowsill and watched to see what happened next.

Witch Upadee took a peacock's feather and stroked the tiny egg. Then she blew on it hard and chanted, 'Grow, grow. Quick and slow. Make yourself sweet for witches to eat. Grow, grow. Quick and slow!'

And, to Sneaky's enormous astonishment, that tiny chocolate egg began to grow big on the plate! How it grew! How it swelled up! My goodness, Sneaky did feel hungry when he saw that great egg of chocolate, all ready to be eaten, growing bigger and bigger! He nearly fell off the windowsill in surprse – and then, what a shock he got! Witch Upadee saw him and gave a shout of rage. She picked up her broom and swept him right off her windowsill!

'You nasty little sneaking thing, always peeping and prying! Go away! You *shan't* see my spells!'

But Sneaky had seen enough. He ran home grinning and rubbing his hands. *He* would make a chocolate egg grow like that, too – and my, what a lot of money he would make by selling it!

He bought a chocolate egg and took it home. He set it on a plate and then went to borrow a peacock's feather from his friend next door. He stroked the little egg with it, and then blew on it hard, feeling tremendously excited. Then he chanted loudly the magic song, 'Grow, grow. Quick and slow. Make yourself sweet for *fairies* to eat. Grow, grow. Quick and slow!'

The chocolate egg began to grow. How it grew! You really should have seen it. It was a most marvellous sight. First it was as big as a hen's egg. Then as big as a goose's. Then as big as a swan's. Then as large as an ostrich's. Then as big as a coal-scuttle – and it went on growing.

Sneaky was delighted. He danced round in joy, watching the egg grow.

It grew and it grew. Crack! It broke the plate with its weight. But Sneaky didn't mind. He could buy lots of new plates with the money for that lovely egg! That the egg grew bigger than the table – and crack! One of the legs gave way, and down went the table and the egg, too. But still it went on growing!

When it was as big as a large wheel-barrow Sneaky thought it was big enough. After all, he had to get it out of the door and take it to market – it wouldn't do for it to get *too* big! So he shouted to it. 'Stop! Don't grow any more, egg!' But the egg didn't take a bit of notice, no, not a bit. It just went on growing – and however much Sneaky begged it to stop it simply wouldn't. Sneaky didn't know the right words to say, you see! Well, it grew – and it grew – and it grew – and at last it couldn't grow any more, because it was as big as the room itself – and poor Sneaky was squashed flat in one corner. And then in pressing itself against the ceiling, the egg broke! Out came a great stream of sticky cream – all over poor Sneaky! After that the egg stopped growing, for the spell was broken.

But do you know – the only way Sneaky could get out of the room was by eating his way through the egg! It took him two days – and oh, the mess he was in! And now, if you meet a small elf who says he simply can't BEAR Easter eggs, just ask him his name. It's sure to be Sneaky!

Chestnut Prickles

Once, when the pixie dressmaker was going home from the Queen's palace, with a bag full of money in her hand, the robber gnomes lay in wait for her. 'She has been paid for all the dresses she has made for the Queen,' they whispered to one another. 'Let us rob her! She is so small and weak, and we can easily take her money.'

The blackbird heard what they said, and he flew to warn the little dressmaker. He sat up in the big chestnut tree and sang to her as she came along. 'Beware, beware! Hide yourself, little pixie! The robber gnomes are lying in wait for you!'

The pixie was frightened. She rushed to the chestnut tree and climbed up on to its stout branches. There she sat, trembling. She hoped the gnomes would pass by, and then she could slip down and run home. But, no – they spied her up in the tree and shouted in glee.

'There she is! We'll wait till she comes down!' They sat around the tree trunk, and the poor little dressmaker was trapped!

She began to cry. The chestnut felt her tears on its leaves, and it whispered to her to comfort her. It tumbled a chestnut down on her lap, dressed in its green, prickly case. She picked it up – and an idea crept into her mind.

'I'll wait till it's dark – then I'll pick lots of these prickly cases – and I'll sew them together with my needle and thread and make myself a prickly coat! Then if I slip down the tree and the gnomes try to catch me, *what* a shock they'll get!'

As soon as it was dark the little dressmaker picked dozens of the prickly chestnut cases. She sewed them together with her strongest thread, and made herself a long coat, right down to her ankles. With four of them she made a prickly cap for her head – and then she was ready! With the prickly coat well wrapped around her, and the prickly cap on her head, she slipped down the tree. The gnomes at once leapt up in the dark and pounced on her.

They caught hold of the pixie – but, dear me, how prickly she was! 'Ooh! Oh! Ah!' cried the gnomes, letting her go at once. 'We're pricked! We're scratched! It's a nasty little hedghog! Let it go. Sit down and wait again, for surely the pixie will climb down soon.'

They sat down – and the pixie hurried home safely with her money, chuckling to think of the trick she had played on the robber gnomes. '*What* a useful coat I made!' she thought. 'How cross the gnomes will be in the morning when they see I'm gone!'

And I should just think they *were*!

The Remarkable Doughnut

There was once a small goblin called Greedy, who was just like his name. He was very fond of doughnuts, and every day he went to the baker's to buy a large brown doughnut for his tea. They were always fresh, and new, and fat little Greedy enjoyed them very much.

One day as he came home he was caught by a band of gnomes and taken off to be their servant. He was very angry, and so afraid that his doughnut would be taken from him that he held tightly to the bag.

The gnomes took him to their cave. They gave him a pail and a scrubbing brush and ordered him to clean the floor. But Greedy was not going to.

'What!' he cried, his little green eyes flashing brightly. 'You think I, a clever goblin, will be slave to a pack of stupid gnomes like you!'

The gnomes flew into a rage and shook the

cheeky goblin till his teeth rattled like dice in a box.

'Ask us anything in the world and we'll tell it you!' they cried. 'Only ask us. *Then* you will see how clever we are!'

Greedy the goblin turned pale. What could he ask them? They were sure to know everything, really, for he knew they were friendly with the witches and shared all their strange and wonderful secrets.

'Go on, go on!' shouted the gnomes. 'Ask us something! Quick! If you ask us something and we know the answer we'll turn you into a wasp without a sting, just to teach you not to be so cheeky another time!'

Greedy thought that if he took a bite out of his doughnut it might help him. So he took it out of the bag. His mouth watered when he saw its round, sugary surface, and he longed to taste the jam that lay hidden in one corner of the doughnut's inside.

And then the great question came to him. *He* knew what to ask those goblins! Of course he did. He held out the doughnut to them and bade them look carefully at it, seeing that there was no hole anywhere at all.

Then he bit it and the dob of jam gushed out. 'Now tell me, o gnomes,' said the little goblin, 'how was the jam put inside the doughnut, for, as you saw, the brown skin of it was whole and had no opening anywhere.'

The goblins crowded round in surprise. One of them took the doughnut and looked at it carefully. 'A most remarkable thing,' he said. 'Now, let me see – how *could* that jam be put inside? Let me see.'

And while they were all puzzling their heads about it Greedy slipped out and away! He had lost his doughnut, but found his freedom. Do *you* know the answer to his question? Think hard, like the gnomes!

The Wrong Side of the Bed

Long, long ago, the wizard Ten-toes bought a marvellous bed. There were dragons carved at the head, with long, coiling bodies, and peacocks with spreading tails carved at the foot. The dragons had eyes of rubies and the peacocks had eyes of sapphire blue, so you can guess how strange they looked with their eyes gleaming in the dark at night. The wizard liked the bed very much, he said it made him feel more like a wizard than ever.

He had bought it from a witch, and when she sold it to him she said, 'Ten-toes, whatever you do, always get out on the *right* side of the bed. If you don't you'll be sorry!'

She wouldn't tell him why, but she knew quite well. A bad-tempered little imp had made the bed for himself. One day the witch had placed a spell upon him, got him into her power and taken the bed for herself. But she could not get rid of the little black imp. He made himself invisible and squatted down beside his beautiful bed, which he would not leave night or day. The witch found it out one morning by getting out on the side of the bed where the imp crouched.

What a shock for her! He bit her foot, and his sharp teeth sent poison into her – the poison of his own bad temper. And that day the witch couldn't do anything right! How she scolded, how she raged! How she stamped her foot and frowned! It was terrible to see.

She sold Ten-toes the bed, but she wouldn't say a word about the invisible imp that went with it, for she was afraid that if she did he would not pay her so much money. The wizard was pleased with the bed. He slept well in it and was careful each morning to get out on the right side.

One day he forgot. He was sleepy and got out the wrong side. He trod on the invisible imp, who at once bit him in a rage. 'Dear, dear!' said the wizard, surprised. 'I must have stepped on a pin!'

All that day things went wrong for Ten-toes. He lost his temper, he shouted and raged. He hit the man who came to clean the windows, he shook his fist at the woman who sold him potatoes. Really, he behaved very badly indeed. The bad-temper poison was working very strongly in him!

The next morning Ten-toes got out the *right* side of the bed and things went well. The morning after he got out the *wrong* side, and everything went wrong again because of his bad temper. He simply couldn't understand it!

He met the witch and frowned at her so fiercely that she was frightened and astonished. Then she suddenly thought of something.

'Did you get out of bed the wrong side this morning?' she called after him. The wizard stopped and thought. Yes, he had! Dear, dear, dear! So that explained his bad temper, did it? What a peculiar thing! Well, he would be careful to get out the *right* side after that!

That was hundreds of years ago! But it's a strange thing, isn't it, that we still say to a bad-tempered person, 'You must have got out of bed on the wrong side this morning!' Now you know how that saying began!

The Stupid Little Girl

There was once a small girl called Eileen who had very good brains, which she was too lazy to use. She couldn't even say her two times table when she was eight years old, so you can guess how lazy she was, because they are *very* easy, aren't they!

'Eileen, why are you so stupid?' her teacher asked her one day. 'You have good brains if only you will use them. You should be at the top of the class, not at the bottom.'

'Well, perhaps it's because I haven't any brothers or sisters,' said Eileen. 'I am an only child, and only children can't help being backward.'

'Rubbish!' said her teacher. 'You'd be just the same if you had half a dozen brothers and sisters, Eileen.'

'Oh, no, Miss Brown. I'm sure I shouldn't,' said Eileen. 'If only someone would give me a brother and a sister I know I'd be different!'

Now, although Eileen didn't know it, a little gnome was listening to what she said. And that evening he tapped at Eileen's window and called to her.

'Eileen!' he cried. 'Come out! Your brother and sister are here and are longing to play with you.'

'Oh!' said Eileen in delight. 'So I've got a brother and sister after all, and didn't know it. How lovely!'

Out she ran into the garden, and the first thing she saw was a big grey donkey, who gravely held up his fore-foot to shake hands with her. Eilen looked at the gnome astonished.

'It's your brother,' said the gnome. 'Shake hands, can't you? He's just as stupid and obstinate as you are, so you and he will get on very well together. He will be a very good brother for you.'

'I don't want a donkey for a brother,' said Eileen, going red. 'How horrid of you, gnome! Where is my sister? I will play with her, and not with this donkey.'

'Here's your sister,' said the gnome, and he pointed to a big goose waddling down the garden. 'She will make you a fine sister. I have often heard your mother call you a silly goose, so I have found a goose to be your sister. Won't you have fine times together, you and the donkey and the goose!'

'I *won't* have a goose and a donkey to play with,' said Eileen in a rage. The goose and the donkey looked at the angry little girl out of solemn eyes.

'Is this the child you said would be our sister?' asked the donkey. 'Well, we don't want her. She looks too silly for anything. We are sure she would be too stupid to play with us. Goodbye, little girl, we will go and find someone more interesting.'

Off they went and the gnome looked at Eileen. 'There you are!' he said, disgusted. 'Even a foolish donkey and a silly goose don't want to know you. You *must* be stupid, even though your teacher says you have good brains!'

'I *have* got good brains!' shouted Eileen, and she ran indoors to do her homework. And you will be glad to hear that she began to use her brains so that in a few weeks' time she was top of her class. It *was* a good thing the gnome tried to find a brother and sister for her, wasn't it?

The Bread and Milk

Binkle the kitten was very fussy one day. He turned up his nose at the nice dish of bread and milk that his owner put out for his breakfast. He wanted fish.

'You shall have fish this afternoon,' said his owner. 'Now eat your breakfast up properly.' But Binkle went away in a corner and sulked. The dish of bread and milk stood in the porch, full to the brim.

Soon the robin spied it. Down he flew and chose a big piece of soaked bread. Four sparrows saw him, and flew down to join him. The robin didn't like eating with other people, so off he flew – and the sparrows pulled pieces of bread about, eating a very good breakfast indeed! Other sparrows heard them chirruping happily and came to join them too.

Then a small mouse peeped out of his hole in the bank not far off, and sniffed with his little woffly nose. How good that bread and milk smelt, to be sure! He really must have a taste! Off he scampered and came to the dish. The sparrows flew off to have a dust-bath, and left the dish to the little brown mouse. He nibbled daintily here and there, and wondered what made the bread taste so very delicious. What a fine breakfast he was having!

A movement under the lavender bush that grew near the door startled him so much that he ran off in a hurry, thinking it might be Binkle the kitten hiding there. But it was only old Prickles the hedgehog, who lived in the garden and ate beetles, slugs, and grubs whenever he could find them. He, too, had smelt the bread and milk and meant to have some.

He ambled up to the dish, tipped it up so that he could drink the milk, and then began to feast. How he enjoyed it!

Just then he heard the pattering of footsteps, and up came Bobs the dog. The hedgehog, who was not afraid of any animal in the world, walked back to the lavender bush and curled himself up there to go to sleep. Bobs knew him well, and left him alone. He sniffed at the dish and licked it well all around.

Now Binkle the kitten began to feel very hungry, and off he went to find his breakfast, thinking that bread and milk wasn't so bad after all – but when he came to the dish it was empty!

'*We* took some,' said the robin and the sparrows, cheekily. '*I* ate some,' said the little mouse, peeping out. '*I* took some,' said the prickly hedgehog, licking his lips. 'And *I* licked the dish,' said Bobs.

'You greedy things!' cried Binkle, in a rage. 'It was *my* breakfast!'

'And ours, too!' said everyone, and *how* they laughed!

The Sulky Sweets

Everybody knew the Sulky Brownie. He was such a miserable-looking creature. He made other people unhappy, and he himself was the unhappiest of all.

Now it is very unusual for any of the Little Folk to sulk, and everyone felt certain that the brownie had caught the disease from someone in our world – for, as you know, there are plenty of boys and girls who suffer from the sulks when they are not very well. So the pixies, the gnomes and the brownies had a meeting about it to see what could be done for the poor sulky brownie.

He wanted to be cured too. A sulky person is so miserable that if he could find a quick and easy way of curing himself he would do so.

'We could ask the old witch Know-all,' said a gnome. 'I live next door to her, and she really is a marvel at curing things.'

'Well, ask her, then,' said the others. So he

went home and asked his neighbour the witch how to cure a person of the sulks.

'That will cost you ten pieces of gold,' said Witch Know-all, greedily. The gnome paid up the money at once. Then the witch grinned and took a packet out of her cupboard. She undid it and showed the gnome some round, flattish white things that looked like sweets.

'These are sulky sweets,' she said. 'If a sulky person takes one of these and sucks them, smiling all the time that the sweet is in his mouth, his fit of sulks will be cured as soon as the sweet is finished. There you are! And the secret is well worth ten pieces of gold!'

The gnome hurried off to the sulky brownie and told him what the witch had said. The brownie was very grateful, for he really did want to be happy, like ordinary people, and get rid of his silly sulking fits. So the very next time he began to sulk, he took the witch's advice. He popped into his mouth one of the sulky sweets and began to suck it. All the time he was sucking it he made himself smile without stopping. The sweet took a long time to disappear – but will you believe it, as soon as it was gone and the brownie thought about his sulks, *they* had disappeared too! Yes, and he felt quite happy. It was marvellous.

But here is the curious thing. *Those sweets were not magic ones at all!* What do you think they were? Just ordinary white acid drops, the sort you buy at any sweet shop! And the very curious thing is that if anyone in *our* world buys those acid drops, and sucks one when he is sulking, smiling all the time, *his* sulks will go too! You might tell this to anyone who sulks, or try it yourself if *you* feel sulky. But don't forget – you must smile all the time the sweet is in your mouth! *I* shan't charge you ten pieces of gold, as the old witch did, but you might let me know if the strange little spell still works!

The Stupid Goblin

One day Snip and Snap the brownies went fishing in the pond belonging to the Red Goblin. They hadn't caught more than three fish when up came the Red Goblin and pounced on them. 'Aha!' he cried. 'I've got you! I'll lock you up in my deep, dark cave!'

He dragged them off, and in a little while Snip began to cry loudly and say, 'I've left my net behind. My nice new net!'

'Well, go back and get it quickly,' said the goblin, crossly, and Snip ran off. But he didn't come back, as you can guess.

'Perhaps he has lost his way and can't find us,' said Snap. 'Shall I go and fetch him?' The goblin let him go – and of course Snap didn't come back either.

The next week those silly little brownies went to gather bluebells in the goblin's wood. Out he pounced and caught them again.

'Aha!' he shouted. 'I've got you again. I'll lock you up safely *this* time.' He dragged them off, howling and crying. Presently Snap clapped his hand to his head and said. 'I've left my cap in the woods. I shall get sunstroke, I know I shall.'

'This is the sort of trick you played on me last time,' growled the goblin, stopping. 'I let one of you go back, and he lost his way. Then when the other went to find him, *he* didn't come back either!'

'Well, let us *both* go back for the cap together,' said Snap. 'Then we shan't lose our way.'

'Go then, and hurry back,' commanded the goblin. 'I will wait here.' Off went the two brownies, and though the goblin waited until midnight, you may guess that neither of them went back! No, they were safely in their beds at home!

In a few days the foolish brownies went to hunt for the first wild rose on the hedge that ran round the Red Goblin's meadows. He was waiting for them and pounced on them in delight, chuckling gleefully. 'I'll lock you up *this* time!' he shouted.

But before they had gone a great distance

Snip began to cry loudly and feel in his pockets one after the other as if he had lost something. 'What's the matter *now*?' asked the goblin, impatiently.

'I've left my purse full of money under the hedge,' wept Snip. 'Oh dear, oh dear, what shall I do?'

'Ho!' said the Red Goblin, stopping and looking slyly at Snip. 'So you're trying to play me that old trick once more, are you? You want to go back for your purse and slip off home again. No, no, brownies, you can't trick an old goblin like me a third time. I shan't let *you* go again – *I* shall go and get that purse while *you* stay here! Ha, ha, that will teach you that I'm too clever for you!'

And off he ran back to the hedge, where he hunted in vain for the purse of money. When he got back to where he had left those two brownies they were gone! Poor old goblin – he wasn't very clever, was he?

The Boast That Came True

Woffles the rabbit was a boaster. He boasted about everything under the sun, and made himself out to be the most wonderful and most powerful rabbit that ever lived.

But there came a day when he boasted once too often, as you shall hear. It happened when a good many animals were all talking together by the pond that lies at the end of a very long field, the other side of Cuckoo Hill. They were chattering busily, when flying through the sky there came a noisy aeroplane.

'Look at that strange bird,' said Prickles the hedgehog, half frightened. 'I hope it doesn't come down here!'

'I could make it come down if I wanted to!' boasted Woffles at once. 'But if it would frighten you, I won't tell it to come down, Prickles.'

'What stories you tell!' said Mowdie the mole,

scornfully. 'As if you could make a great bird like that come down into our field. You are a silly boaster, Woffles!'

'I tell you I *could* make it come down,' said Woffles at once. 'It's only because it would frighten Prickles that I don't tell it to come here.'

'Stuff and nonsense!' said Mowdie. 'Prickles, go down my hole and hide. Now, Woffles, Prickles has gone. Tell that big bird up there to come down and we'll see if you are telling the truth or just boasting as usual.'

'Yes, go on!' cried all the others, pleased to see Woffles looking rather red.

Well, what could Woffles do but tell the aeroplane to come down? He cleared his throat and then said boldly, 'Strange, noisy bird up there in the sky, come down to our field!'

To everyone's enormous surprise and alarm the aeroplane began to circle round and come lower and lower. The pilot had been told that he must land on this long, flat field, and wait for two other aeroplanes to join him there. So down he came!

R-r-r-r-r-r-r-r-r-r! What a noise the engine made as the aeroplane dropped lower and lower.

Then at last it landed on the grass. All the animals were rooted to the spot, frightened out of their lives, not daring to move or to cry out in case the strange big birds with widespread wings should eat them up. Then to their horror, two more of these queer creatures appeared in the sky, and they too began to circle over the field and come down.

With squeaks, shrieks and squeals every animal fled into ditch, hole, and hedge, scared out of their lives. And the one who ran the fastest of all was Woffles the boaster! He fled into the deepest tunnel he knew of and crouched there, hardly daring to move.

'Woffles, Woffles!' someone called, suddenly. 'Where are you? Come and tell those horrible birds to go away. You made them come and you must make them go.'

But Woffles wasn't going to put his nose into that field again, not he! He crept away down another tunnel and was soon miles away, on the other side of Cuckoo Hill. And from that day he was so afraid that what he said might come true that he never once boasted again!

Sly-One is Caught

There was a reward offered in Oak-Tree Wood to anyone who could catch the thief Sly-One. He was a green goblin, cunning and quick. He liked to lie in wait for pixies and elves going through Oak-Tree Wood and pounce on them. Then he would rob them of their money.

The pixie Nimble longed to catch Sly-One. Nimble hadn't much money, and he lived with his pet hedgehog in a very small cottage. One day he sat on his stool and thought of a plan to catch Sly-One. He told it to Prickles his hedgehog, and Prickles agreed.

The next thing that Nimble did was to send a message to his cousin, Niggle, to say he would be bringing him some money on Friday night. He gave the message to Chatter the magpie, and of course, Chatter told the message to everyone in the wood before he took it to Niggle. Sly-One the goblin heard the message and grinned to himself. He would hide in the hazel bush near Niggle's house and as soon as Nimble came up with the money he would jump on him and get it. It would be dark so Nimble wouldn't spy him.

But Nimble sent for Hush-Hush the owl, and begged him to follow Sly-One on Friday night, find out where he was hiding, and come back to tell him. So when Friday night came Hush-Hush followed Sly-One on his silent wings and saw him hiding himself in the hazel bush. He flew back to Nimble and told him. Then Nimble chuckled and told Prickles the hedgehog.

They set off through the wood together. But when they came near the hazel bush Nimble told Prickles to go in front and make as much noise as he could. So on went the hedgehog, shuffling through the leaves, loudly.

Sly-One thought it was Nimble. He leapt out from the bush and flung himself heavily on top of Prickles. Ooh! What a dreadful shock! Pins and needles! Tacks and nails! Whatever had he fallen on?

Nimble rushed up with a torch, and how he laughed to see the green goblin stuck fast on the hedgehog's hundreds of prickles! 'Hold him,

Prickles!' said Nimble, chuckling. 'We've got him now! You can carry him to Oak-Tree Town just like that.'

Off they went, though Sly-One struggled and begged for mercy. It was no good. The thief was caught. As soon as the folk in Oak-Tree Town knew what had happened they all turned out to see the goblin stuck on the hedgehog. How they laughed!

Nimble got the reward, and now he is so rich that he and Prickles have treacle pudding for dinner every day. Aren't they lucky!

Timothy's Tooth

Once upon a time a long, long while ago, the fairies were making a spell in a big cauldron over a fire of blue flames. It was a good spell and a wonderful one – a spell to make sick people better. All the pixies and elves bent over the steaming cauldron and watched the colour in it change from red to orange, from orange to yellow, yellow to green, from green to blue – and dear me, then it stopped! Now that was quite wrong, because the enchanted liquid should change through all the colours of the rainbow, it shouldn't stop at blue! It should go on to indigo and then to violet, when the spell would be finished and perfect.

'Ooooooooh!' squealed the elves, in their little high voices. 'We've missed out something!'

'Ooooooooh!' cried the pixies. 'What shall we do?

Then there was a rush for the big Magic Book

that belonged to the Queen, and a great rustle as the thick pages were turned over. A small pixie found the place and read out loud.

'To make the spell perfect one small white tooth should be added; a child's tooth is best.'

All the little folk looked at one another sadly. 'We shall never get that,' they cried. 'Never! How could we go round pulling out children's teeth?'

'Wait!' said an elf. 'I know a little boy called Timothy, who is very kind. He might give me one of his teeth if I asked him.' So off he flew to Timothy. He told the little boy all about his difficulty, and Timothy listened.

Timothy was seven years old. One of his first teeth was very loose indeed. He often waggled it to and fro with his finger, but he wouldn't let his mother take it out, though he knew it wouldn't really hurt. He liked to feel it waggling. But if the elf wanted it to finish the wonderful spell; why certainly Timothy would give him the tooth.

'As soon as my mother comes in I'll ask her to take out my loose tooth for you,' promised Timothy. The elf gave him a hug. 'Will you put it under your pillow when you go to bed tonight?' he asked. 'I'll come and get it when you're asleep – and for payment you can have a wish that will come true – and perhaps some money too, if I can get some for you!'

Well, Timothy's mother took out the tooth and it didn't hurt a bit. Timothy slipped it under his pillow – and, will you believe it? the next morning the tooth was gone, and a bright shining coin was there instead. Timothy's wish came true, and he was so excited and happy that he told everyone what had happened. The news soon spread, and to this very day, if you put your little white tooth under your pillow, you will find it gone in the morning, and maybe a coin there instead. Don't forget to wish a wish too, will you!

The Four-leaved Clover

A four-leaved clover is very lucky! If you find one and keep it, it will grant you a wish, so the pixies say – and they ought to know, because they make them grow.

One day a small girl called Nora found a four-leaved clover in a field. She was so pleased. She picked it very carefully and looked at it. Yes, it had four little leaves instead of three!

'Now I can have a wish,' thought Nora. 'I know what I shall wish for – that lovely doll in the toyshop window. I've wanted it for ever so long!'

She skipped off, the four-leaved clover in her hand. On the way home she met Tommy and Joan, hand in hand, crying bitterly.

'Our mother's ill and she's gone to hospital,' wept Joan. 'We want her back.'

'Perhaps she won't be long,' said Nora, putting her arms round the children.

'We can't do without her,' said Tommy. 'She puts us to bed each night and gives us our dinner when we come home from school. What shall we do now she's gone?'

Nora was very sorry for the two unhappy children. She knew how horrid it was when mothers went away.

'Look!' she suddenly said to Joan and Tommy. 'I've found a four-leaved clover, and a wish belongs to it. I was going to wish for that big doll in the toyshop window – but if you like, you can wish for your mother to come home tomorrow,' she said.

'Oh, thank you, Nora – you *are* kind!' cried Joan. 'I'll come and tell you when our mother comes home.'

Nora left them and went home. She hadn't seen a lady standing nearby, waiting for a bus. She hadn't known that the lady had heard every word and had thought Nora was one of the nicest children she had ever seen.

The lady went to Tommy and Joan and asked where Nora lived. Then she went to the toyshop and bought the very big doll that sat in the middle of the window. She wrote a little note and put it inside the box in which the doll was packed. Then she asked the shopwoman to send the doll by post to Nora's house, addressed to Nora.

Early next morning Tommy and Joan came running round to Nora's house, their faces beaming bright. 'Our mother is coming home today! The hospital say there's nothing wrong with her! The clover wish came true! We've brought it back again in case you want to wish with it, too.'

'But a clover leaf only has one wish,' said Nora. 'It's no use now. I *am* glad your mother's coming home. Oh, look, here's the postman with a parcel – and it's for *me*!'

It was a very big doll! There was a note, too, that said, 'The clover leaf you found had *two* wishes, you see!'

'Well!' said Nora, astonished. 'Just think of that! Oh, how lucky I am!'

Ah, but she deserved it, didn't she!

Tuppy and the Goblins

Tuppy was a gnome. He was short and round and fat, and he looked after a sack of gold for the Prince of Here-we-are Land. One night he fell asleep instead of doing his duty and the green goblins came and stole the sack of gold.

What a to-do there was! The Prince stamped up and down, and shouted and raged, and Tuppy shook like a leaf in a storm.

'Go and get back my gold or I'll turn you into a caterpillar and throw you to the birds!' cried the Prince. So off went Tuppy like the wind.

The goblins lived at the top of Twinkle Hill. Tuppy climbed up the hill, and crept into a cave near the top. He spied a big round barrel lying on its side there. 'This will make me a fine hiding place!' thought Tuppy, and he crept inside.

He was tired with his climb and he fell asleep. When he woke up it was night and he heard voices. He peeped through a hole in the barrel and saw the green goblins sitting in a ring, talking. In their midst was the sack of gold they had stolen from the Prince. Oh, how could Tuppy get it?

The goblins were quarrelling loudly. Suddenly one of them ran to the barrel in which Tuppy was hidden and dragged it forward with Tuppy still inside. The goblin wanted to stand on it to make himself heard. He stood the barrel upright and jumped up. Tuppy was inside, very much frightened. He heard the goblin dancing about on top, shouting loudly, and he didn't like it. He thought they knew he was in the barrel, and were going to punish him in some dreadful way.

'I shan't stand it!' thought poor Tuppy, shaking and shivering with fear. 'I shall walk away, barrel and all!'

So he began to walk off, and the barrel, of course, went with him. The goblin on top of it fell off with a bang and cried out in surprise and fear. Tuppy went on, the bottom of the barrel bumping against the ground as he walked. It was heavy and very uncomfortable. The green goblins stared in astonishment and alarm when they saw a barrel walking along. Tuppy couldn't see where he was going and he bumped into first one goblin and then another, knocking them all over.

'Ooh! Ow!' they cried, and took to their heels and fled down the hill! Tuppy bumped along, as frightened as the goblins themselves. The barrel over him looked most strange and peculiar as it went along, looking for all the world as if it were walking on its own!

When Tuppy heard no more noise he guessed that the goblins had gone, and he wriggled out of the barrel. In great delight he saw the sack of gold nearby. He stuffed it into the barrel, turned it on its side again, got in it himself, and rolled down the hill! Over and over he went, and the running goblins cried out in terror as he bumped through bushes and hedges, rolling over their toes and sending them flying. 'What is it, what is it?' they cried.

Tuppy wasn't turned into a caterpillar. The Prince was so pleased with him that he made him Chief Taster of Puddings in the Royal Kitchen, and Tuppy is now so fat that he couldn't get into a barrel if he wanted to! He *does* love to tell about his adventure with the goblins. Can you pretend you are Tuppy and tell it too?

The Five Lost Beans

Once there was a small boy called Thomas, and he was very pleased because he had five, hard, polished beans which his teacher had given him from one of the bean-bags at school. It had burst open, and the children liked the shiny purple beans very much. So each child had been given a few.

Thomas put his beans into his pocket, and let them rattle together there. They were nice to feel and nice to hear. He took them with him wherever he went. One day he went to play in the garden, and he and Micky the dog played at policemen and burglars, which was most exciting. First Micky was the policeman and Thomas the burglar. Thomas had to hide somewhere, and Micky had to find him. Then it was the other way about. Micky was really very good at playing games.

Once when he was the burglar Thomas went

to hide right at the bottom of the garden by the rubbish-heap. And while he was crouching there all the beans fell out of his pocket. Thomas was so excited at watching for Micky that he didn't notice them – and when, later on, he found that all his shining beans were gone, he was very disappointed. He hunted for them, but he couldn't find them anywhere.

'Never mind!' said his mother. 'You'll find them one day, I expect!'

But Thomas didn't find them, and soon he forgot all about them. The winter went by, and the springtime. Summer came – and one day his mother was in a great fix. Thomas's uncle and aunt were coming to dinner, and the green-grocer hadn't sent the peas! It was Wednesday, and the shops would soon be closed. There would be no time to fetch the peas!

'Go and see if there is a marrow growing on the rubbish-heap!' called Thomas's mother to him. 'There may be one big enough to cut.' Off went Thomas down to the rubbish-heap, where the marrow plants always grew – but there was no marrow ready.

And then – dear me – he caught sight of something else. Growing up the fence there were some runner beans, full of red flower at the top – and crowded with fine green beans at the bottom! Thomas stared at them in astonishment. Nobody ever planted beans there. However had they come? He didn't wait long to wonder. He rushed indoors, fetched a basket and ran down to the bottom of the garden again. Soon he had picked a fine basketful of tender green beans, and took them to his mother. How pleased she was!

'Where did you buy them, Thomas?' she asked. 'They will be lovely for dinner.'

'I didn't buy them,' said Thomas. 'They are growing at the bottom of the garden, Mother – five fine runner beans. Who could have planted them?'

'I know!' said his mother, laughing. So do I. Do you?

The Wishing Balloon

Once upon a time Chitter the gnome found a yellow Wishing-Balloon with its string caught in a bush. He was delighted, for he guessed it had blown away from some witch. Oh, wouldn't he have some fun wishing wishes with it!

He took it and went on his way home. Soon he met his friend Twink, and he thought he would show off a bit, for Twink had no idea that the yellow balloon was a magic one.

'Hallo, Twink,' he said. 'You look cold. What's the matter?'

'I wish the sun would come out,' said Twink, shivering. 'I *do* feel cold.'

'I'll bring it out for you!' said Chitter, grandly. 'I wish the sun would come out!' At once his wish was granted, and the sun shone out warmly. Twink gaped at Chitter in surprise.

'Ooh, are your wishes coming true this

morning?' he asked. 'Do wish some more, Chitter!'

'I wish for a bag of chocolates for myself and a bag of sweets for you,' said Chitter at once. In his hand appeared a fat bag of big chocolates, and in Twink's hand came a small bag of sweets. Twink was disappointed. He wanted chocolates too.

'You *are* mean, Chitter,' he said. 'I'd like chocolates, too.'

'You'll just have what I wish for you,' said Chitter, crossly. 'Now I'll wish for something else. I wish for a fine red motor car for myself and a blue bicycle for you!'

At once a little red motor car, shining and new, appeared beside him, and by Twink came a pretty blue bicycle. Chitter climbed into his car and tooted the horn proudly. But Twink threw his bicycle roughly down on the ground.

'You are mean and selfish!' he cried to Chitter. 'You wish all the best things for yourself, and not nearly such nice things for me. Wish me a motor car, too.'

'No!' said Chitter. 'You can have the bicycle.'

'I *won't* have it!' said Twink, and he stamped on a wheel and broke it.

'Oh, you horrid, ungrateful gnome!' cried

Chitter, in a temper. 'I just wish you'd fall into a bed of nettles!'

Poor Twink! The next moment he found himself in a clump of nettles and he howled as the leaves stung him. He jumped out, ran up to Chitter and smacked his cheek. Chitter jumped out of his car in a rage and hit Twink on the nose. Then they fought like two little tigers. It was dreadful to see them. In the middle of the fight a wind blew up and off went the yellow Wishing-Balloon, floating in the air. It blew against a prickly holly bush – Pop! It burst and that was the end of it. Chitter heard the pop and looked round. Oh, his lovely Wishing-Balloon!

He began to cry, and then he told Twink what had happened. The two silly gnomes sat and wept. The car, the bicycle, and the sweets had all vanished when the balloon burst. Now they had nothing at all.

'If only we hadn't quarrelled!' sobbed Chitter. 'Perhaps we'll find another Wishing-Balloon some day. Then we'll be more sensible.'

I'm afraid they'll *never* find one!

The Little Stickleback

There once lived a tiny stickleback in a little round pond. He was very happy, for the water was warm, and there was plenty of company for him. The water-beetles always had something to say, the tadpoles wriggled by, chattering, and the newts were always willing to stay and talk.

One day a sparrow came to the pond to drink. She was very happy, and as she sipped the water she chirruped loudly. 'Why are you so glad?' asked the stickleback, swimming up.

'I am happy because I have built myself a lovely nest in a gutter,' said the sparrow. 'And I have laid five eggs there, and soon they will hatch. Then I shall have little ones to look after, and that will be most exciting.' The sparrow flew away. The fish swam off, thinking. He met a newt and the newt spoke to him. 'What are you thinking about, Stickleback?'

'I am thinking of making a nest and getting

a wife to lay eggs there for me,' said the stickleback.

How the newt laughed! He called the tadpoles, the water-spider and the beetles, and he told them what the fish had said. Then they all laughed loudly.

'Whoever heard of a fish making a nest?' said the newt. 'You're a funny fish, Stickleback!'

All the same, the stickleback meant to do as he said. He swam about and found tiny bits of stick, which he took in his mouth. He put them all together in a cosy corner. He found some bits of grass, too, and put those with the sticks, glueing them together. Soon he had made a queer little nest, like a muff! It had two entrances, just as a muff has!

Then he looked about for a nice mother-stickleback. He soon found one and asked her to lay some eggs in his nest. She didn't want to at first, but he chased her into the nest and wouldn't let her go out until she had laid a little batch of eggs. But the stickleback didn't think there were enough, so he waited till he saw another mother-fish, and then he chased her, too, till she went into the muff-like nest and laid a few more eggs.

The stickleback thought he had enough. He was very proud of his nest and eggs. He called the newt and the tadpoles to come and see it. They laughed – but if they came too near the stickleback went red with anger and chased them away, all his little spines sticking up straight!

He loved those eggs. He used to float himself into the nest and stay over them. Sometimes he nosed them gently, turning them over. At other times he waved little currents of water over them by working hard with his fins just nearby.

When the eggs hatched into tiny fish the stickleback was so excited! The nest seemed rather a tight squeeze then, so what do you think he did? He took away the top of it! Then it looked much more a like a bird's nest, for it had no top. If another stickleback came near to look at the fish the little father swam straight at him, red with rage.

The baby fish learnt to swim. They swam away from the nest – but if a big water-beetle came along, back they went in a hurry, their little father keeping guard. He *was* proud of his children.

'Well, you may all laugh at me if you like!' he

said to the tadpoles and the newts. 'But I did what I wanted to, and my baby fish are well and happy!'

I wish you could see them! They are all in my pond, as happy as can be, and the father stickleback is the proudest fish in the garden!

Who? Who? Who?

One night there was a great to-do at the court of the pixie Princess, Sylfai. Her crown had been stolen! She looked on her bed, she looked in her wardrobe, she even looked in her shoe cupboard, but there was no shining crown to be seen. Someone, someone had stolen it!

But who? Sylfai didn't know, and her servants ran here and there, hunting and searching, crying, 'Who is the thief? Who has taken the crown?'

Then it was decided that a messenger should be sent out all over the land crying out that the thief must be found. He must be sent that very night. But who should the messenger be?

'We must have someone with a big voice,' said Sylfai, 'and it must be someone who can see in the dark, and can fly quickly.'

'I know!' cried an elf. 'Let's send the brown owl! He has a very big voice, he always flies at night, and he can see everything.'

So the big brown owl was sent for and he came silently flying on his soft wings.

'Go out over the woods and fields and find out who has stolen my crown,' said Sylfai. So he flew off into the darkness, and nobody heard his wings as he went. But they heard his voice, for it was very loud.

'Who?' he cried. 'Who? Who? Who?'

The gnomes in the hills, the elves in the fields, and the brownies in the wood all ran out trembling with fear to hear this strange question shouted through the night.

'What do you mean?' they cried. 'Why do you shout "Who?" like that?'

'*Who* has stolen Sylfai's crown?' shouted the owl. 'Who? Who? WHO?'

Suddenly he came to an old tree. Once upon a time the owl had nested there, for the hole in it was a deep one, well suited to an owl's dark nest. The owl went to peep in it, wondering whether his old nest was still there.

He looked down with his big staring eyes, and saw a small pixie there, called Tvit. 'Who?' cried the owl, remembering his errand. 'Who? Who? Who? WHO?'

'Oh!' shrieked Tvit the pixie, frightened out of his wits. 'Oh! What do you mean?'

'*Who* has stolen Sylfai's crown?' shouted the owl. 'Who? Who? Who?'

Tvit tried to scramble away from the queer, big-eyed creature looking down at him, and as he moved the owl caught sight of something shining. It was the lost crown! Tvit had stolen it!

The owl was filled with delight. He picked up the frightened pixie in one claw, and the crown in the other. Then he flew straight back to Sylfai, calling, 'Who? Tvit! Who? Who? Tvit, Tvit!'

Sylfai was delighted, and gave the owl a gold ring to wear on his ankle as a reward. He was so pleased with his cleverness in finding the crown that he still goes round each night calling the news to everyone. Have you heard him? 'Who?' he cries. 'Who? Who? Tvit, Tvit! Who? Who? Tvit!'

Listen and you're sure to hear him!

Good Old Jock!

Jock was the school dog. He was a little black Scottie dog, with short legs, a waggy tail, and sharp, cocked ears. His eyes were soft and brown, and all the children loved him and petted him.

And how he loved the children! His tongue worked hard, licking their hands and legs. He stood at the school gate each morning waiting for the children to come running up when Miss Brown rang the school bell. He barked to each child, and they all gave him a pat. Some of them brought him biscuits, so he was a lucky dog.

He really belonged to Miss Brown, the teacher, but she shared him with the children. He lay quietly in the classroom while lessons were going on. He had to be turned out in the singing lesson, though, because he wanted to sing, too! And his voice was not the kind that Miss Brown liked!

Now one Saturday morning a horrid thing happened to poor Miss Brown. She was coming down the stairs when she slipped and fell. And when she tried to get up she couldn't! She had hurt one of her legs very badly.

'Oh, dear!' said Miss Brown. 'Whatever am I to do? I must get help somehow. I can't lie here all day.' But there was no way to get help, because no one else was in the schoolhouse. No children came on Saturday. Miss Brown groaned in dismay. What *could* she do? Then up came Jock and yelped in surprise to see his mistress lying there, he licked her and pulled at her skirt.

'It's no good, Jock, I can't move,' said Miss Brown. 'Can you go and get help? Run out of the school gate and bring someone back with you.' Jock understood quite well. He rushed out of the door into the playground. But the school gate was shut! Jock jumped up – but his short little legs were no good at all for jumping! Now what was he to do? If only he could get his friends, the children! Jock could never understand why there were two days of the week when the children kept away. He was always miserable on Saturdays and Sundays. Jock sat down and thought hard. How could he get the children?

Then into his clever doggy mind came the picture of the school bell! What did Miss Brown do when she wanted the children? Why, she rang the big bell, shaking it by its wooden handle! Jock sprang up, his tail wagging. If only he could get the bell from the table!

He managed to get on the table. He pushed the bell with his nose and it fell to the floor with a clang. Jock picked it up by the wooden handle and ran out into the playground. He ran round with it in his mouth, jumping up and down, ringing the bell with all his might.

The children in the village heard the bell and stared in surprise. 'Miss Brown wants us!' they said, and they tore off to the school. You can guess how surprised they were when they saw Jock jumping about the yard, ringing the bell!

It wasn't very long before Miss Brown was found. One of the children fetched her mother and the doctor, and soon Miss Brown was comfortably in bed.

And what a fuss everyone made of good old Jock! But, really, I do think he was clever to ring that bell, don't you?

The Very Old Kettle

Once there was a fine, shiny kettle that lived on the kitchen fire and sang a song every time it boiled. It had boiled water for thousands of teapots and hundreds of hot-water bottles. And then one day when Mother looked into it she saw that there was a hole in the bottom. 'So that's why you make a sizzly noise on the stove!' she said. 'You are leaking. What a pity! You are no good any more. You have done well, but now you must be thrown away.'

The kettle was sad. It loved the bright kitchen. It knew everything in it so well. It didn't want to be put into the dustbin for the dustman to collect. It didn't feel at all old or tired. But as Mother was going to put it into the dustbin Gillian and Imogen came along. 'Oh, Mummy! Can we have that old kettle to play at houses?' asked Gillian. 'We have a pretend house under the hedge at the bottom of the

garden. It will be lovely to have a kettle for boiling water when we pretend to have our tea.'

So Mother gave them the kettle to play with and the kettle was happy. What a fine time it had with Gillian and Imogen! They filled it with water from the tap in the garden and set it on a pretend fire to boil. They filled their doll's teapot with the water. The kettle tried to sing, and it felt glad to be with the two happy children. Bobs the dog came along, too, and sniffed at the kettle. He even drank out of it when he found the water inside was cold. That pleased the kettle very much.

But after a time Gillian and Imogen got tired of playing houses. They left the kettle under the hedge and forgot all about it. They played Red Indians instead. The kettle was lonely and forgotten.

'This is worse than being in the dustbin!' thought the kettle. 'No one comes near me. I am getting rusty and my hole is much bigger. There are spiders' webs inside me. I shall never never be any use again. And yet I don't feel old or useless!'

One day a cock robin came to the kettle. He put his head on one side and looked inside. He called to his mate: 'Here is a fine place for a nest! Look! This kettle will shelter us and our eggs well. It is a good kettle.'

How pleased the old kettle was! It tried to sing as it used to do, to tell the robin how happy it would be if they would build inside it. It wasn't long before the robins began to tuck grass-roots, dead leaves, bits of moss, and many other things inside the kettle! They made a beautiful nest and lined it with hairs that Bobs had shaken off his coat. Then they laid their four pretty eggs there.

And now the kettle is happy all day long. The hen robin sits in the nest and talks to it. The cock robin brings his wife tit-bits and sings. Soon the eggs will hatch, and how pleased the old kettle will be to feel the tiny creatures inside it, safe and sheltered!

How do I know all this? Well, you see, the old kettle and the robins' nest are in my garden! I see them every day as I walk down the path!

Brer Rabbit Plays
Blind Man's Buff

Now one Christmas-time Brer Wolf gave a party
and he asked Brer Rabbit and Brer Turkey
Buzzard, Brer Terrapin and Brer Fox, Brer
Wildcat, Brer Bear, and Brer Mink, and a whole
lot of others. Everybody came, and played party
games.

Brer Rabbit was skipping round as merry as
you please, looking as plump as a Christmas
turkey. He won the game of musical chairs, and
he always saw the thimble first. Brer Fox, who
thought himself pretty smart, was angry with
Brer Rabbit. He looked at him, so plump and
merry, and thought he could make a fine meal of
that cheeky Brer Rabbit. Brer Rabbit, he
hopped around in time to the music, wearing a
fine yellow crown that he had got out of a
cracker, thinking he was king of the party.

'Now we'll have a game of blind man's buff,'
suddenly said Brer Fox, winking at Brer Wolf.

Brer Wolf saw that Brer Fox had a plan of his own and he winked back. 'Right!' he said. 'Will you be blind man first, Brer Fox?'

'Yes, Brer Wolf,' said Brer Fox. Brer Wolf took out a large white handkerchief and went to tie up Brer Fox's eyes – but Brer Rabbit stepped up and took it. 'I'll tie up his eyes!' he cried. 'I'm good at tying, Brer Wolf!'

Brer Fox was wild. He wanted Brer Wolf to tie his eyes up because he knew Brer Wolf would leave him a crack to peep out of – but Brer Rabbit, he tied the handkerchief so tightly that Brer Fox couldn't see a thing! Then the game began. Of course, Brer Fox meant to catch Brer Rabbit, and he listened for the patter of his paws and always went after him. And pretty soon Brer Rabbit guessed what Brer Fox was up to and he ran over to Brer Wildcat.

'Change caps with me, Brer Wildcat,' he said. 'I've been king long enough. It's your turn now. I'll have your bonnet.'

No sooner had they changed than Brer Fox managed to catch Brer Rabbit, but when he felt the bonnet on his head instead of the crown, he let him go! And not long after that he caught old Brer Wildcat. He was about the size of Brer

Rabbit – and he wore the crown, too – so Brer Fox was certain he was Brer Rabbit all right!

He picked him up and ran into the passage outside with him. He bit at a whisker – he nibbled at an ear, which seemed very short for Brer Rabbit! He snapped at the tail – and then, dear me, Brer Fox got the shock of his life! For Brer Wildcat lashed out with his twenty claws and Brer Fox let him go at once!

'Stop it, Brer Rabbit, stop it!' cried Brer Fox. 'I was only having a joke.' Brer Wildcat shot into the garden, every hair on end – and Brer Rabbit slipped out into the hall in his place. So, when Brer Fox tore the handkerchief off his eyes, he didn't see Brer Wildcat at all, but Brer Rabbit, looking as calm as could be.

'My, Brer Rabbit, what made you fierce like that?' said Brer Fox, looking at all his scratches. 'I was only having a bit of fun.'

'My, Brer Fox, and so was I!' said Brer Rabbit, and he skipped off as merry as a blackbird. After that Brer Fox kept out of his way, though he couldn't help wondering how it was that Brer Rabbit was wearing a bonnet now, instead of a crown! Poor old Brer Fox – he can't trick Brer Rabbit, can he?

The Birthday Kitten

It was Peter's birthday – and will you believe it, all he had was one card, and one present! Peter lived with his Aunt Sally, and she wasn't very fond of small boys, and didn't really know what they liked. So Peter's one present was a new pair of socks – and socks aren't at all exciting, are they, for a birthday?

'I did so want that big book of adventure stories in the bookshop,' thought poor Peter, as he pulled on his new socks.

Peter went to school as usual, and because it was his birthday the children clapped their hands eight times for him – he was eight, you see – and he liked that very much. On the way home he saw something under a hedge, and he looked to see what it was. At first he thought it was a big grey mouse.

But it wasn't. It was a tiny tabby kitten! Peter couldn't think how it had come there, for there was no house near. It was mewing, for the weather was cold, and the kitten was hungry. Peter was kind and he bent over the tiny creature.

'You poor little thing!' he said. 'I can't leave you here. I shall take you home under my coat.' So he popped the tiny creature inside his coat – it did feel nice there – and ran home with it. Aunt Sally was not pleased to see it. She said Peter could only keep it if it lived outside in the shed.

So Peter made it a warm bed there, and fed it every day himself. The kitten grew and grew. It became fat and sleek. It purred loudly. It loved Peter very much and always ran to welcome him home from school.

One morning the schoolteacher said that, for a treat, the children should have a pet show. They could each bring their pets, and she would look at them all, and see which was the best cared-for. So, of course, Peter brought his cat along, too. It was still a kitten, but big and fat, and its striped fur was as soft as silk.

It was fun that day at school. Ellen brought her canary in its cage. John brought his dog and so did George. Mary took her white rabbit and

Doris had a tortoise, but it was asleep in its box for the winter, and they didn't wake it. Harry had a cat and so had Nellie. And, of course, Peter had his kitten, which he said was his birthday kitten because he had found it on his birthday.

The teacher looked hard at every animal and bird. She said they all looked well-cared-for and happy. But when she came to Peter's tabby kitten, purring loudly and looking so fat and silky and sleek, she really couldn't help picking it up to stroke it.

'Peter, your kitten wins the prize!' she said. 'She is simply beautiful – quite perfect! I can see you love her and look after her well. Go and fetch the prize from the table.'

And what do you think the prize was? Guess! Yes – it was the big book of adventure stories! Peter was so delighted – he had got what he wanted after all!

'You are a real birthday kitten!' he said to his cat. 'You have brought me the birthday present I so badly wanted!'

The Three Hunters

Leslie, Allan, and Mollie had a holiday because it was Saturday. So they were out in the lane with their little dog Joker.

'Let's pretend to be hunters!' said Leslie. 'I've cut myself this stick from the hedge. It will do for a spear!'

'And I've made myself a wooden sword!' said Allan.

'And I've got my bow and some sticks for arrows,' said Mollie. 'What shall we hunt?'

'Let's hunt the cows in the field, and pretend they are lions,' said Leslie.

'But the farmer wouldn't like us to chase his cows,' said Allan. 'We must only *pretend* to hunt them.'

'All right, we'll just pretend,' said Leslie. 'We'll creep through this hole in the hedge and spring out on the lions!'

'I believe there are some tigers there as well!'

said Mollie, fitting an arrow to her bow.

'And I can see a spotted leopard!' whispered Allan, drawing his sword. 'Come on – we'll hunt the wild animals and not be a bit afraid of them!'

They all squeezed through the hedge, Joker the dog, too. The cows pulled at the grass and didn't even bother to look at the children creeping round them – but, dear me, when Joker the dog began to prance round the cows didn't like it at all. They didn't trust dogs!

'Moooooo!' said one cow, in such a loud voice that the children jumped.

'That was a lion roaring!' whispered Allan. 'Come on – we are three of the bravest hunters in the world!'

They went nearer – and so did Joker. But that was too much for the quiet cows. They all lifted their heads and stared hard at the dog and the children.

'Moooo, moooo!' bellowed a cow and took a step towards Joker.

'MOOOOOOOOO!' roared another cow suddenly and put her head down to run at the dog. It looked exactly as if she was going to run at the children, for Joker was nearby them.

Leslie, Allan, and Mollie stopped and looked

at the cows. 'I don't believe they like being lions and tigers and leopards,' said Mollie. 'They look angry.'

'Moooo-oo-oooo!' said a cow in front, and Mollie jumped in fright. She dropped her bow and arrows and ran for the hedge. Allan dropped his sword and ran, too, and Leslie followed, still keeping his stick in case the cows attacked them! But as soon as the cows saw Joker the dog running off, too, they put their heads down peacefully and went on eating.

The children squeezed through the hedge and almost fell into the lane! And there, standing watching, was Mr Straws, the farmer! How he laughed when he saw them!

'Are you hunting the cows or are the cows hunting *you*?' he said. 'Dear me, I didn't think my harmless old cows would send you scrambling off like this!'

Leslie and Allan and Mollie went red. They didn't feel very brave after all.

'You go and hunt for late blackberries,' said Mr Straws, kindly. 'There are plenty in my field on the hill. You'll be quite safe hunting for blackberries – they won't bellow at you and send you running home.'

'Thank you very much!' said the children, and off they ran on another hunt!

Pitter-Patter's Dance

There was once a mischievous little pixie who loved to peep and pry. His name was Pitter-Patter, and this was because he had such nimble, pitter-pattering feet. If you have heard the raindrops pitter-pattering on the window-pane in a shower, then you will know what the pixie's feet sounded like as he ran here and there.

One day, going through the wood, Pitter-Patter came across two boys lying asleep under the trees, for the sun was hot and the boys had walked a long way. The pixie took a grass and tickled their noses. They sneezed loudly and woke up. Pitter-Patter tried to escape behind a bush – but the bigger boy reached his hand out quickly and caught him!

'Oho, so it's a pixie!' said the boy, in surprise. 'I didn't think there were such things! Look, Bill – a real live pixie! I'm going to tie him up with a bit of string so that he can't get away.'

In a flash he had tied Pitter-Patter's feet and hands together so that the pixie couldn't move. The two boys sat and looked at the little fellow. He glared back at them, and begged to be set free. But the boys wouldn't untie him.

'No,' said Bill. 'You're a great find. We'll take you to school tomorrow, and give our class the biggest surprise in their lives!'

'I shall bite and scratch if you pick me up!' said Pitter-Patter angrily.

'Well, I saw a cardboard box thrown down by some untidy person in the woods as we came along,' said Bill. 'I'll go back and find it, Ted, and you keep your eye on this pixie till I come back. Then we'll put him in the box and take him home in that.'

Bill went off. Pitter-Patter looked at the boy who was left. Then the pixie began to whistle – and he could whistle beautifully, just like a blackbird and a nightingale rolled into one!

'I say!' said Ted. 'I wish I could whistle like that! My word, you *are* clever!'

'You should see me dance though!' said the pixie. 'When I whistle, and dance to my whistling, my feet make a pitter-pattering noise like the rain, and you can hardly see them move, I

dance so nimbly. Ah, it's a sight to see me dance! The little folk pay a great deal of money to see me dance.'

'I'd like to see you, too,' said Ted.

'Well, untie my feet, then, and I'll dance for you till Bill comes back,' said Pitter-Patter. 'You can leave my hands tied.'

So Ted untied the pixie's feet, and Pitter-Patter began to dance. How he danced! He kicked up his feet, he pattered them on the ground like sticks on a little drum, he twisted and he turned, and all the time he whistled till Ted's eyes nearly dropped out of his head!

Pitter-Patter danced to a bush and back again. He danced to the oak-tree nearby – and back again – and then he danced all round the bush – and all round the tree – and danced off down the path – and danced through the wood – and danced right away and away!

So when Bill came back with the box, there was Ted looking very foolish indeed – and no pixie! Ah, you see, it needs sharp wits to outdo the fairy folk. *You* might have let that pixie go, too!

Well, Really, Amelia!

Have you a good memory? I hope you have, because it is a very useful thing. Amelia had no memory at all – and usually she didn't try to remember anything, either!

Now one day her mother had to go to see the doctor, so she left Amelia in charge of the house.

'Now listen, Amelia,' she said. 'You must remember to do *three* things for me. Sweep out the yard. Water the lettuces. And, if it rains, bring in the washing.'

'I don't think I shall remember them, Mother,' said Amelia, looking worried.

'Well, you must,' said her mother. She looked at Amelia and saw that she had three big buttons down the front of her dress. She went to her work-basket and snipped off three pieces of white tape. She tied one piece to the top button. 'This will remind you to sweep out the yard,' she said. She tied a second piece of tape to the second button. 'And this will remind you to water the lettuces. And this third piece will remind you to bring in the washing if it rains!'

Amelia was pleased. She said goodbye to her mother, and then settled down to read her book. After a while her eye caught sight of the second piece of tape, tied in a bow on the second button. She frowned. 'Now what was that for?' she said. 'Let me see – something about watering, wasn't it? Oh, yes – water the hens, Mother said!'

Amelia thought she had better get on with the jobs while she remembered them. So up she jumped, filled the water-can and went to the yard. Soon she was watering all the hens, much to their astonishment.

'I expect it is to make you grow,' said Amelia, pleased. She looked down at the first button with its bow of white tape. 'Now what was that one for?' she wondered. 'Something to do with sweeping, wasn't it – oh, yes – sweep out the washing yard! Good!'

She got the big broom and began to sweep out the yard where all the clean washing was blowing in the wind. What a dust she made! All the dirt flew up and down and soon the clean washing was smutty and black!

She looked at the last piece of tape and frowned. Whatever was it for? Oh – rain! Yes! She had to bring the lettuces in if it rained. She looked up at the sky, and a few drops of rain began to fall, for the clouds were very low. 'I must bring in the lettuces!' said Amelia. So off she ran to the lettuce-bed and cut the lettuces there.

'Now I can untie all these tape-bows,' said Amelia.

But when her mother came home, how cross she was! There was the washing out in the pouring rain, looking wet and surprisingly dirty! There were the hens in a dirty yard, all of them looking surprisingly wet! And there, on the kitchen table, were two dozen fresh lettuces!

'Well, really, Amelia!' began her mother – but Amelia was nowhere to be seen! She had suddenly remembered three things when she saw her mother's cross face. One was that her mother could get very cross indeed. The second was that it would be better to find a good place to hide. And the third was that if she didn't go quickly it would be too late!

The Brownie and the Witch

Once upon a time Snip the brownie found a yellow toadstool with a blue stalk. He was very pleased, because yellow toadstools with blue stalks have a great deal of magic in them, and Snip thought he could use the magic for making all kinds of spells.

But Deep-one the witch heard of his find, and sent to say she would like to buy it. Snip sent back a note to say that he wasn't going to sell it – and that made Deep-one as angry as could be. So she lay in wait for Snip the brownie, and one day as he was on his way home from marketing in the next town, she jumped out at him from behind a tree.

'Good afternoon, Snip,' she said. 'I want your toadstool.'

'Well, you can't have it,' said Snip, 'because I haven't got it on me! You don't expect me to wear it for a hat or use it for a shoe button, do you? It's at home.'

'Don't be cheeky to *me*,' said Deep-one, in a
rage. 'I know you've got it at home. I'm coming
home with you – and I'm going in at your door –
and I'm going to take that toadstool from its
hiding place!'

'Oh, you are, are you?' said Snip, thinking as
quickly as a rabbit can run.

Deep-one took hold of the brownie's arm very
tightly so that he couldn't run away. Then Snip
pretended to be very frightened. He went on
through the wood, thinking, thinking, thinking
what he could do to save his wonderful yellow
toadstool. He came to the end of the wood. He
went up the lane and round by the poppy field.
He went up the hill – and halfway up he came to
a dark little cave running into the hill-side.

A curtain of bracken grew around the
opening, and a carpet of moss led to the cave.
'So this is where you live,' said Deep-one. 'Well,
I shouldn't choose a dark little cave like this, but
I've no doubt *you* like it! Now, whereabouts do
you keep that toadstool? You'd better tell me, or
you'll be turned into a blackberry on a bush.'

'Please, Deep-one,' said the brownie, 'go
right in. You'll find a door at the back. Open it,
and take the clock off the mantelpiece. You may

find the toadstool behind the clock – if you are lucky!'

The witch went into the cave – but Snip didn't go with her! No – not he! That wasn't where *he* lived! It was the cave of the Ho-Ho Goblin! And the Ho-Ho Goblin didn't like visitors at all – especially those that came in without knocking and took the clock off the mantelpiece!

Snip hid behind a tree to see what would happen – and it wasn't long before he saw quite a lot of things! The witch Deep-one had walked into the cave, opened the door at the back, and had gone straight to the little mantelpiece in the room beyond.

She hadn't seen the Ho-Ho Goblin there – but he had seen Deep-one – and with a roar of rage he jumped at her, shouting, 'Thieves! Robbers! Burglars!'

The bad-tempered little goblin caught up his broom and swept the witch off her feet! He swept her out of the door! He swept her out of the cave! Down the hill she went rolling over and over, in the most terrible fright, for she really didn't know what was happening at all.

As for Snip the brownie he laughed till he

cried, and called out to the witch, 'Didn't you find the toadstool behind the clock after all? Well, well, well!'

And after that Deep-one left Snip alone – he was much too smart for her!

Grunt! Grunt!

Jack and Doris wanted to go blackberrying. They knew that the best hedges for blackberries were in the farmer's fields, but they were not allowed to go there unless they asked politely at the farm. So they took a basket each and went off to the farmhouse.

'Please,' said Jack to the farmer's wife, 'may we go into the fields and pick blackberries?'

'Certainly,' said the farmer's smiling wife. 'But see that you shut the gates as you go, and don't frighten any of the animals, or chase the ducks.'

'We'll remember,' promised Jack and Doris. They went off through the farmyard to the fields. The farm was a big one. There were cows in one field, horses in another, and sheep in another. Pigs grunted not far off, and geese cackled by a pond. Along the stream-side sat a row of white ducks, basking in the sunshine, and hens ran everywhere, clucking and squawking. Jack and Doris loved the farm and all the fields around.

They went past the pigs' field and into the next one. Here was a high hedge, black with ripe juicy berries. What fun! Jack and Doris began to eat them as fast as they could. There would be plenty left to fill their baskets, too.

'Oh, look, Jack! Here are the biggest blackberries I've ever seen!' said Doris. 'Let's stop eating, and fill our baskets with them. Mother will be so pleased to see such lovely ones. She will be able to make a fine pudding with them!'

So they filled their baskets full. How nice they looked, brimming over with the ripe berries! The children set them down on the grass, for they were heavy. They went a little way up the hedge to look for more to eat.

And then they heard a strange sound! Grunt! Snort! Grr-unt! They looked round. Five big pigs had come into the field and had run up to the baskets of blackberries! A pig upset Jack's basket, and began to gobble up the berries!

'Oh! Oh!' cried Jack, in a rage. 'Go away, you naughty pigs! Go away!'

But the pigs took no notice at all. They upset

the other basket too, and before the children could save their lovely blackberries, not one was left! Then the pigs came running to the children for more, and sniffed and snuffed round their legs in a most alarming manner. They did not mean to hurt them, for they were quite harmless, friendly animals, but they did like those blackberries, and wanted Jack and Doris to get them some more!

Jack began to shout loudly. 'Go away! Go away!' Doris began to cry big tears all down her cheeks.

The farmer's wife heard their shouts and cries and came running to see what was the matter. The children told her.

'Dear, dear!' said the farmer's wife, very sorry. 'What a pity! Look – someone has left the field-gate open, so that the pigs wandered in from the next field. I wonder who was silly enough to do that.'

Then Doris and Jack went very red. 'Oh, dear, I'm afraid we forgot to shut the gate,' said Jack, in a small voice. 'It's all our own fault!'

'Well, you will know better next time,' said the farmer's wife. 'Come again tomorrow – and remember to shut the gate!'

Brer Rabbit Plays Ball

Once upon a time Brer Rabbit looked over the wall that ran round Brer Fox's garden, and he saw a plum tree there, full of the finest yellow plums he had ever seen.

'My!' thought Brer Rabbit to himself. 'Maybe Brer Fox would offer me a few of those plums if I go and ask him how he is! I could do with some plums, for it's a thirsty morning!'

So he opened the gate and went to Brer Fox's house, swinging his stick and whistling a little song. But no sooner was he at the door than Brer Fox put his head out of the window and said:

'I guessed you'd be along this morning, Brer Rabbit – and I guessed right. As sure as I've got fish in my larder, honey in my cupboard, and plums on my tree you come along just as saucy as a jay-bird. Well, I'm not opening my door to you – and if you don't get out of my garden pretty quick I'll jump out of this window and get you!'

'Now, now, Brer Fox,' said Brer Rabbit, in a hurt voice. 'Who cares about your plums? I've come to show you my fine new ball. I thought maybe you'd like a game.'

He took a brand new ball out of his pocket. Brer Fox opened the door and had a look at it. It certainly was a fine ball – red, yellow, blue, and green – and it bounced so hard that it caught Brer Fox under the chin and made him bite his tongue almost in half!

'Come out and have a game of catch,' said Brer Rabbit. 'Brer Bear told me no one could beat you at catching a ball, Brer Fox.'

So Brer Fox went out into the garden with Brer Rabbit. But first he said, 'Now, no asking me if you can have plums off my tree, Brer Rabbit.'

And Brer Rabbit said, 'What! Has your tree got plums on? Well, well, well, fancy me not seeing those! No, Brer Fox, I won't ask you for a single plum. Plums always upset me at this time of year. Catch!'

He threw the ball so suddenly that Brer Fox missed it, and it went over the wall. Brer Fox gave a grunt and jumped over to get it – and just as he bent down to pick it up, Brer Rabbit made a grab at the plum tree and picked two ripe plums! He put them into his pocket and then held his paws ready to catch the ball when Brer Fox threw it.

Brer Fox caught the next three balls and Brer Rabbit praised him up to the skies till Brer Fox felt he was as clever as twelve foxes rolled together. But then Brer Rabbit threw another high ball, and over the wall it went! And over the wall went Brer Fox – and into Brer Rabbit's pocket went two more plums! So it went on, till Brer Rabbit's pockets were so full he couldn't put any more plums into them at all!

'Well, Brer Fox, I guess I'll be going now,' said Brer Rabbit at last. 'Thanks for the game of ball. It was fine!'

And when he got halfway down the road he yelled out, 'And thanks for the plums, too, Brer Fox! Mighty nice plums they are, just ready for eating!'

Then Brer Fox took a look at his plum tree – and he jumped over the wall and made after Brer Rabbit as fast as ever he could. But Brer Rabbit was down a burrow, laughing as hard as can be at his wicked game of ball!

The Little Bird

There was once a little bird who told tales about other people all day long. He was a perfect little nuisance!

When he perched on Dame Winkle's windowsill one morning, he saw her putting on her shoes – and dear me, she had a big hole in her stocking. So he flew all round the town that day, whispering in people's ears, 'Dame Winkle has a hole in her stocking!'

Another day he saw Snip-Snap the brownie climb over into the next-door garden and pick up some apples. The little bird flew off, and all that day he told his tale to everyone he met. 'Snip-Snap took some apples that didn't belong to him!'

Nobody was safe from that little tale-teller! He peeked in at windows, he pried into every corner. Many people tried to smack him when they saw his pointed beak poking round the

corner – but he was always just a bit too smart for them!

And then one day he told a tale about Goggins the witch. He had flown down into her garden one afternoon and seen her sitting in a chair having a snooze. He had hopped nearer – and nearer – and nearer. And then he had noticed a shocking thing – Witch Goggins hadn't washed her neck! Dear, dear, dear! He flew off in delight and soon he was telling the tale all over the town. 'Witch Goggins doesn't wash her neck! Fancy that! Witch Goggins doesn't wash her neck!'

Now it was a rule in that town that everyone should wash properly, and as soon as Mr Blueboy, the policeman, heard what the little bird whispered in his ear, he marched off to Goggins and scolded her sternly. The witch said she was very sorry, and asked who had told Blueboy the news.

'That little bird,' said Blueboy, pointing to where the little bird was sitting on the wall, listening. Witch Goggins went indoors to wash her neck, and she vowed to herself that she would catch that little bird and punish him!

But do you suppose she could get near enough

to that cunning little bird to catch him? No, she certainly could not! He flicked his wings and flew off as soon as he saw her. He wasn't going to be caught by Witch Goggins! She would probably turn him into a fly and then send a spider along to eat him!

At last Witch Goggins prepared a little can of water to throw over him, and in it she put a spell to make that horrid little bird invisible. She thought that if no one could see him, nobody would ever listen to his tales. She hid behind a curtain and waited.

And at last she got him! He flew down to peep in at the window to see what he could spy – and the witch flung the enchanged water over him. At once he disappeared! The spell had worked.

But do you know, although he couldn't be seen he still had a voice! And he still went about perching on people's shoulders and whispering tales in their ears! He didn't dare to stay in Fairyland any longer, in case Goggins the witch really caught him the next time. So he came to our world, and he still goes on telling tales.

Sometimes people know something you would rather they *didn't* know, and when you say to them, 'How did you know?' they say,

'Aha! A little bird told me!' Then you know that nasty little tale-teller has been in *your* house – but you'll never see him because he is still invisible!

The Bunch of Carrots

Ronald was pleased and proud. He had grown some lovely young carrots in his garden, and today he had pulled them all up, washed them carefully, and tied them into a bundle. He was going to market to sell them.

'Aha!' said Ronald, trotting down the lane to catch the bus to market. 'I shall get at least two pounds for my bunch of carrots. Imagine that!'

He came to the bus-stop, which was by a gate that led into a field. The bus was not in sight. There was no one to talk to but an old grey donkey who leaned his head over the gate and stared at Ronald. Ronald turned his back on him and went on thinking about his bunch of carrots.

'If I get two pounds for my new young carrots, I shall buy two old wheels from the ironmonger and put them on to that wooden box I have at home,' said Ronald. 'That will make a fine cart. Then I shall go to Mrs Brown and Mrs Jones and Mrs Hughes and Mrs Mack and tell them I will do their shopping for them and bring it home in my cart for two pounds a week each.'

He waved his bunch of carrots in the air and went on planning his plans. The donkey stared at him and wondered who this little boy was, talking away to himself. But Ronald took no notice of him.

'In no time at all I shall have about five pounds,' he said. 'I shall buy a hen at the market for five pounds and it will lay me an egg every day! I shall sell the eggs and soon I shall have ten pounds. Then I shall buy a little pig and fatten it up. I shall sell it for fifty pounds when it is big enough. Fifty pounds! I *shall* be rich then!'

He stood and thought for a moment. 'What shall I do with fifty pounds? I shall buy a donkey! I can get one for fifty pounds. Not a silly old creature like this one that keeps staring at me here – no – a nice fat young donkey that will take children for rides on the sands. I shall charge fifty p a ride – no, a pound, I think! Oooh!'

Ronald stood up straight, looking very proud. 'I shall buy myself a new suit with long trousers.

I shall buy a fine hat and wear it just a bit on one side of my head. I shall buy the biggest and best marbles in the toy shop. I shall get that fine blue top that everyone wants – the top that spins for twenty minutes without stopping. And do you think I shall let Tom and Dick and Leslie and Jack play with my marbles or my top? No – I shall point my finger at them and say, "Go away! I don't want to play with dirty little boys like you!"'

Ronald stuck his chin into the air and threw out his hand as if he were telling people to go away. But in his hand was his bunch of carrots – and it so happened that he stuck them just under the donkey's nose!

The grey donkey was pleased and surprised. He thought Ronald was giving them to him. He opened his mouth and took the carrots. Crunch! They were most delicious!

'Oh! Oh!' shouted Ronald, swinging round in a fury. 'You wicked donkey! You've eaten my carrots! Oh, my lovely wheels – my little pig – my pretty donkey – my new suit and hat – my marbles and top! You've robbed me of them all!'

'Hee-haw!' said the donkey, galloping away still munching. 'You've only yourself to blame!'

Little Miss Dreamy

Do you know anyone who really seems half asleep and dreams the day away? I expect you do, because people are always saying, 'Wake up!' to the dreamy person! There may even be one in your class!

This is the story of a dreamy little girl called Jenny. Whatever she was doing she always seemed to be thinking of something else! Her mother used to get so cross with her at mealtimes, because Jenny *would* sit and dream, instead of eating her dinner.

'Jenny! Wake up!' she would say. 'You will never grow big and strong if you don't eat your dinner properly!'

'What will happen to me then?' asked Jenny.

'Oh, you'll grow small instead of big!' said her mother. 'Your clothes will get too large for you – you will look a funny little thing and everyone will laugh at you! Now, do eat your dinner!'

That afternoon at school the teacher told the children that they were to change their cloak-rooms. The big children were to use the small children's cloakroom to hang up their hats and coats and keep their shoes – and the small children were to use the big cloakroom. The change was made because there were more small children than big, and so they were to have the bigger room.

'I will show each of you your new peg and the hole for your shoes,' said Miss Brown. 'Please remember them or you'll get into a muddle. Jenny, wake up! Do you see your new place in this cloakroom?'

'Yes, Miss Brown,' said Jenny.

But, will you believe it, when afternoon school was over, Jenny ran off to the *old* cloak-room and went to her old peg and hole! She quite forgot that it belonged to a big child now! She took the hat and coat off the peg and changed her shoes, putting on those in the hole. Then off she went home.

But, dear me! The coat belonged to a much bigger child and so did the school hat! So did the shoes – so before long Jenny felt most uncom-fortable! The coat nearly reached the ground!

The hat slipped over her nose and she couldn't see! The shoes slopped all over the place – and the gloves she tried to put on were no use at all!

All the children passing by laughed at her. She really did look so funny! Jenny stood still and looked down at herself! Why were her clothes so large – they seemed to be falling off her!

The little girl gave a cry of fright.

'I've gone small! Mother said it would happen if I didn't eat my dinner! It's come true! I'm growing down instead of up! Oh, oh, what shall I do?'

She ran home crying as if her heart would break. Mother wondered whatever was the matter – and when Jenny told her how she had gone small, and her clothes didn't fit her any more, she began to laugh – and laugh – and laugh!

'You silly little dreamer!' she said. 'You have someone else's clothes on! Whatever will you do next? You are just the same size as usual – but you have taken a bigger child's clothes!'

Jenny got into trouble over that, for Miss Brown was very cross. But she *was* glad she hadn't gone small after all, and you can guess that she made up her mind not to dream any more!

Brer Fox's New Suit

Once upon a time Brer Bear sent out invitations to a picnic party. Brer Fox had an invitation and so had Brer Rabbit, and everyone else. They were all as excited as could be.

Now Brer Fox had a fine new suit, and he longed to wear it. Brer Rabbit had a new suit, too; but he didn't think he could very well wear it at a picnic. He thought maybe people would only wear old clothes at a picnic party. He wondered if Brer Fox would wear his grand new coat and trousers. Brer Rabbit hoped he wouldn't, because Brer Fox's new suit was much grander than his.

Now, when the day came, Brer Rabbit decided to put on his old clothes. It was a fine sunny day, and he thought there would be races and rolling on the grass. So he put on his old blue trousers, his rather dirty coat with a patch in one elbow, and his hat that had been sat on by mistake once or twice. Then he set off down the road, lippitty-clippitty.

But Brer Fox put on his fine new suit. It was very grand indeed. It had green trousers with braid down each leg and a yellow coat with silver buttons. Oh, Brer Fox felt mighty fine in his new suit! He set off down the road, swinging his stick.

And then he saw Brer Rabbit – in his oldest clothes – grinning away as if he saw something mighty funny in Brer Fox and his new suit!

'Are you going to *town*?' asked Brer Rabbit. 'I thought you were going to Brer Bear's picnic to play hide-and-seek and run races and all that.'

Brer Fox felt silly in his new suit when he heard all this talk of races and games. He scowled at Brer Rabbit, turned on his heel and went home again. He took off his nice new suit and put on his old brown trousers and his old coat and cap. Then he set out once more.

And what about Brer Rabbit? Ah, no sooner did that artful rabbit see Brer Fox trot home to change his suit – than *he* trotted home, too, to change *his*! He meant to put on his *new* suit now and make old Brer Fox feel simply dreadful!

He slipped into his nice new things. He

waited until Brer Fox had gone down the road again and then he walked out, as smart as a newly minted coin!

Brer Fox was a bit late – and he found, to his horror, that Brer Buzzard, Brer Terrapin, and all the rest were in their best things, and so was Brer Bear! 'Still,' thought Brer Fox, comforting himself, 'Brer Rabbit will be in *his* oldest things – so I shan't be the only one!'

But when Brer Rabbit turned up he was smarter than anyone there, in his beautiful trousers and coat! Brer Fox stared at him in horror and dismay. Brer Rabbit had played *another* trick on him!

Brer Fox didn't enjoy the party one bit. He felt so dreadful in his old clothes. Brer Bear was cool to him, too, and said loudly to Brer Rabbit, 'It's a pity people can't take the trouble to clean themselves up a bit when they come out, isn't it?'

'It is indeed,' said Brer Rabbit, grinning at Brer Fox. 'I wouldn't ask Brer Fox another time, Brer Bear.'

'You wait till I catch you!' Brer Fox hissed to Brer Rabbit.

'I'll have to wait a mighty long time for that,' said Brer Rabbit. 'Oh, a *mighty* long time, Brer Fox!'

The Two Cats

Once upon a time there were two cats. One was a beauty, with long blue-grey fur, a thick, bushy tail, and great yellow eyes. She was called Princess, and thought a great deal of herself.

The other was a little cat, black, with a little white shirt-front, green eyes, and rather a skimpy tail. Her name was Tibs.

Tibs lived in the kitchen. Princess lived in the drawing-room. Tibs had a raggedy old cushion in a wooden box for a bed. Princess had a round basket lined with blue, and a velvet cushion to sleep on. Tibs ate out of a broken kitchen dish. Princess had a lovely blue bowl with her name all round the edge.

One day the master of the house said that he had lost a great deal of money. He would have to sell his horse. He would have to tell his gardener to go. He would have to buy cheaper clothes to wear and cheaper food to eat.

'You, too, wife,' he said, 'will have to go without things for a little while, until I make some more money for you. How many cats do we keep? Could you not do with one?'

'Well, I only keep two,' said his wife. 'But certainly one would do. I will help you all I can.'

Now, Princess, the beautiful cat, heard all this, and she yawned. 'Ha!' she thought. 'This will be a shock for that common little kitchen cat! She will have to go! Then I shall be the only cat in the house! I will tell her this very day.'

So, when Tibs came padding along to say good morning, Princess told the little black cat the bad news.

'Mistress is only going to keep one cat now,' she said. 'You will have to go. Well, no one will miss you, an ordinary little thing like you, always smelling of rats and mice!'

Tibs was sad. She loved her home. She loved the fat old cook who so often let her come on her knee at night. She loved her raggedy cushion in the wooden box by the kitchen fire. She drooped her skimpy tail and ran away, moping.

The mistress went to the kitchen. She told the cook what the master of the house had said.

'We must only keep one cat now,' she said. 'It

will have to be Princess, of course.'

'But why, Madam?' said the old cook, in surprise. 'What good does that cat do? It eats expensive food, it wants care and fussing – and it never does a bit of work for its living. Yes – I know she's beautiful – but that's no excuse for not working! Look at Tibs, now! She only gets a few scraps a day – but that cat works as hard as I do! She catches mice and rats by the dozen. She never lets one come *near* the larder to eat the things I store there! She saves you pounds and pounds!'

'Dear me!' said the mistress. 'You are quite right. Tibs is too valuable to give away. We will keep her and Princess must go. Tibs works hard for us and deserves her home.'

What a shock for Princess! She was packed into a basket one day and sent away for good! But, as for Tibs, the little kitchen cat, she is there still, happy and busy working hard all night long!

'I'd rather be busy than beautiful!' she says to herself. 'People think much more of you!'

Little Suck-a-Thumb

Once upon a time there was a nice little girl called Hilda. She was clean and neat and pretty, and she had such a kind heart that everyone loved her, even the fairies that lived at the bottom of her garden.

But, although she was quite a big girl, she had such a funny habit – she sucked her thumb! When she was thinking hard, or doing nothing, or going to sleep, her thumb popped into her mouth, and she sucked it hard! She had always done this ever since she was a baby, and her mother couldn't cure her of the funny habit.

'Does your thumb taste nice?' she used to say to Hilda. 'Are you making a good meal of it, my dear? I don't expect you will want any dinner, will you?'

Now it didn't really matter when Hilda was very small, except that it made her nice front teeth grow a bit crooked – but it did look rather dreadful to see her busily sucking her thumb when she grew bigger! Her teacher scolded her, her mother scolded her, her friends laughed at her – but still Hilda went on sucking that little pink thumb of hers! And then one day something cured her. Just listen!

Hilda's birthday was coming near and the fairies thought they would give her a present. So they held a meeting about it and thought of many things. Then a small fairy spoke up loudly.

'Hilda loves to suck her thumb – but it can't be very nice to suck. If it were made of toffee or liquorice it would be much nicer for her! Let's change her thumb into something sweet and she will have a fine treat each day, sucking it.'

So they worked a spell, and when Hilda awoke on her birthday and put her thumb into her mouth to suck, she *did* have a surprise! It tasted sweet! It looked a bit funny, too, because it was made of toffee – a little toffee thumb! How very queer!

Hilda sucked it again. Yes – her thumb really *was* made of toffee. How nice! The fairies must have planned this surprise for her. The little girl sucked away and enjoyed her thumb very much.

But, goodness me, when she next took it out of her mouth, she got such a shock! She had sucked half her thumb away! Yes, really! It did look odd. And what use would it be if she sucked it all away? She wouldn't be able to do up her buttons – or her shoes – or write – or do her handwork! Hilda stared at her tiny thumb in dismay. This wouldn't do at all!

She dressed and ran down to the bottom of the garden. The fairies were there waiting to wish her a happy birthday – but Hilda burst into tears.

'You have spoilt my thumb!' she wept. 'I have sucked it nearly all away!'

'Oh, dear, we didn't think of that!' cried the fairies in a fright. 'Never mind – we'll make a new thumb grow each day – a candy one tomorrow – and a liquorice one the next day – and . . .'

'I don't want sweetie-thumbs!' wept Hilda. 'They are all right to suck, but no use for anything else. I want my own thumb back.'

So they gave her back her own little pink thumb. She was so glad. Do you suppose she sucked it after that? No, she didn't! And she says if you know anyone who sucks his thumb just tell him what happened to hers. So don't forget it, will you!

Lazy Kate

'Kate! Time to get up!' called Mother. Kate was fast asleep in bed. She grunted, but didn't open her eyes.

'KATE! You'll be late for school!' cried Mother.

'She always is,' said John, Kate's brother, sitting down to breakfast. 'She just simply *won't* get up!'

It was quite true. Kate was the laziest little girl you ever saw! Sometimes her mother ran upstairs, and pulled all the bed-clothes off Kate to make her get up – but even then she would go on sleeping, though she had no blankets on her!

'I don't know what to do with her!' said her mother, in despair. 'So lazy and slow – it's really dreadful. She will never be any use to anybody!'

One morning a very strange thing happened. Mother went to call Kate as usual. No answer. She called again. Still no answer. She ran into the bedroom and shook Kate by the shoulder. Kate grunted and turned over the other way.

'Do get up, Kate!' said Mother. 'It's prize-giving day at school today and you mustn't be late!'

'All right, Mother,' said Kate, without opening her eyes. Her mother thought she would really get up now, so she went down to give John his breakfast. But Kate fell fast asleep again!

Then the strange thing happened. Her bed began to groan and creak, and to mutter to itself! Kate took no notice. The bed lifted up one of its feet and put it down again. It grunted loudly. Kate didn't hear.

Then the bed lifted up another foot – and this time it took a step towards the door! Goodness! What a funny thing to happen! Kate's bed was very small, and it got through the door with a squeeze. Then, very carefully, it made its way downstairs, carrying Kate with it! She was dreaming peacefully, and didn't even stir!

Right down to the bottom of the stairs walked the bed, and then, as the front door stood wide open, out it went! Nobody heard it, for the dining-room door was shut.

Down the street walked the bed, carrying Kate under the bed-clothes! How everyone stared! The children were going to school, and they ran after the bed in delight.

'Look! Look! There's a bed walking – and there is someone in it! Oh, what fun! Where is it going?'

Well, it was taking Kate to school! What do you think of that? Just as the bell stopped ringing, and all the children were standing in rows – in walked the bed at the door!

The children squealed and shouted in delight. 'Look, it's come to school! Oh, do look! Who is it in bed?'

They made such a noise that Kate woke up in a fright. She sat up and rubbed her eyes – and then, how she stared – and stared – and stared! Then she went very red indeed, for she felt ashamed to have come to school in her night-dress, and in *bed!* She lay down under the bed-clothes and pulled them over her red face. Oh, dear, oh, dear!

The bed wouldn't walk home again – it liked school so much – so a van had to be fetched to take it and lazy Kate back home.

And do you suppose Kate was ever late again?

No – as soon as that bed gives so much as the smallest creak Kate is out on the floor, dressing!

Are any of you sleepyheads? Be careful your bed doesn't behave like Kate's!

Well, Really, Brer Rabbit!

One day Brer Rabbit went by Brer Fox's house and smelt a fine smell of fresh-caught fish. He stood still and sniffed. Brer Fox poked his head out of the window and grinned. 'Ho!' he said. 'Don't think you'll get *my* fish, Brer Rabbit! I'm up to all your tricks now!'

Brer Rabbit didn't say anything. He walked on, and when he came to Brer Bear's house he sniffed a most beautiful smell there of fresh-picked onions. Brer Bear saw him sniffing and looked out of the window. 'Sniff away, Brer Rabbit!' he said. 'That's all you'll get of *my* onions – just the sniff!'

Well, Brer Rabbit scowled and walked on. Pretty soon he did a little dance, and then ran off to his house. He hunted about until he found a nice long piece of string. He coiled it up, took up his ruler, and went off again. He knew quite well that Brer Fox and Brer Bear would be coming along that way soon to do their marketing – and he just hung about and waited till he saw them. Didn't he get busy then! He measured this and measured that, and then unrolled his string, and looked about as if he wanted something.

'Heyo, Brer Rabbit,' said Brer Fox, strolling up. 'What are you doing?'

'I'm thinking of building a house just here,' said Brer Rabbit. 'I'm just wondering how much ground I'll need. See here, Brer Fox, you might just hold the end of this string for me while I measure out the ground.'

Well, Brer Fox didn't see a mite of harm in that and he took the end of the string. Brer Rabbit went some way off, and then walked behind a big bush. He waited for a moment and then spied old Brer Bear ambling along with his basket. 'Heyo, Brer Bear,' said Brer Rabbit, raising his hat politely. 'Would you be good enough to hold the end of this string for me just a moment? I'm doing a bit of measuring, and it's difficult to use my ruler and hold the string too.'

'All right,' said Brer Bear, and he took the end of the string. Brer Rabbit ran round the bush, disappeared under another one – and ran chuckling through a burrow he knew very well indeed.

Brer Fox stood and held the string for ten minutes or more. Then he grew tired and tugged it. Brer Bear, who was at the other end, felt the tug and tugged back, for he, too, was growing mighty tired of waiting so long. Brer Fox, thinking it was Brer Rabbit at the other end, tugged again – and Brer Bear, feeling cross, tugged back hard. Then first one tugged and then the other, and they both got very angry.

'Stop it, I tell you!' roared Brer Fox.

'Stop it yourself!' shouted back Brer Bear. Then they both began to walk in a rage up the string – and when they got to the big bush they met face to face!

'What are *you* doing holding this string?' growled Brer Fox in amazement.

'Well, what are *you* doing?' grunted Brer Bear, astonished. 'It was Brer Rabbit who gave it to *me*.'

'Well, but why did he do such . . .' began Brer Fox – then he stopped and let out a fearful howl.

'My fish!' he cried, and shot back home.

'My onions!' yelled Brer Bear, and trundled off at top speed.

But it was too late. Their larders were empty, and far away in the wood sat old Brer Rabbit, grinning away as he ate the finest meal he had had for weeks. Well, *really*, Brer Rabbit, whatever will you do next?

Little Black Bibs

Long, long ago, Mother Chinky used to hold a New Year's party each year sometime in the month of January. To it she used to ask the cock and hen chaffinches, the cock and hen robins and the cock and hen sparrows.

There was a big tea of crumbs and small sugar biscuits, which everyone enjoyed. Then there were games, and after that a bran-tub, into which each bird dipped his beak and took out a present. There was one present for everybody, so you can guess it was a big bran-tub.

First the cock robins used to line up and peck out a present each. Then the cock chaffinches and then the cock sparrows. After that it was the turn of the hens. But the strange thing was that there never seemed to be enough presents! There were always some little sparrows who had no present at all because the bran-tub was empty when it came to their turn to peck. They would put their beaks excitedly into the bran, and peck it about hopefully, trying to find a present – and there wouldn't be a single one left!

It was very strange! Mother Chinky really couldn't understand it. She counted the birds. There were forty-eight – and she knew quite well she had put forty-eight presents into the tub. What in the world could have happened?

It was one of the little cock robins who told her at last.

'Mother Chinky!' he whispered. 'It's the little cock sparrows who take too many presents. You see, they first of all take one present each, when they line up as cock sparrows – and then the naughty little creatures line up again with the *hen* sparrows and find presents a second time. So you see there are never enough presents for the last sparrows of all.'

Mother Chinky listened and frowned crossly. The naughty little cheats! The cock and hen sparrows were so much alike that of course she would never notice whether the cocks did come twice or not. It was easy to see that the chaffinches didn't, because the cock had a bright pink breast and the hen hadn't. The robins never cheated, so although they looked

just alike Mother Chinky was sure they would
never play such a trick.

But the sparrows – ah, those cheeky, rude
little birds with their loud voices and pushing
ways – yes, it would be just like them to cheat.

'Still, I like the noisy little creatures,' said
Mother Chinky to herself. 'I want them to come
to my party. But I must certainly stop them
cheating! Now, what can I do?'

She thought of a splendid idea the next year.
What do you think she did? Why, as the
sparrows pushed into her little house, she stood
at the doorway with a pot of black paint – and
she gave each cock sparrow a bib of black as he
passed her!

Then, when the time for the bran-tub came, it
wasn't a bit of use the cock sparrows lining up
again, with the hens, to peck out a second
present for themselves. No! They could easily
be told by their black bibs – and for the first
time there were really enough presents for
everybody.

People say that Mother Chinky still gives her
New Year's party each January, but whether she
really does or not I don't know. The strange
thing is that cock sparrows always appear with

black bibs under their chins then, so perhaps she does! You might look at your sparrows and see if you can tell cocks from hens now. If you can, you'll be as clever as Mother Chinky!